THE SECRET OF THE INDIAN

T H E
SECRET
O F   T H E
INDIAN

LYNNE REID BANKS
ILLUSTRATED BY TED LEWIN

For Ruth Danckert
and the writers of the
Springfield Letters

CONTENTS

THE SECRET OF THE INDIAN

1.

A Shocking Homecoming

When Omri's parents drove home from their party, his mother got out in front of the house while his father drove around the side to put the car away. The front-door key was on the same key ring with the car key, so his mother came up the steps and rang the bell. She expected the baby-sitter to answer.

There was a lengthy pause, and then the door opened, and there was Omri, with Patrick just behind him. The light was behind him too, so she didn't see him clearly at first.

"Good heavens, are you boys still up? You should have been in bed hours ag—"

Then she stopped. Her mouth fell open and her face drained of color.

"Omri! What—what—what's happened to your *face*?"

She could hardly speak properly, and that was when Omri

realized that he wasn't going to get away with it so easily this time. This time he was either going to have to lie like mad or he was going to have to tell far more than he had ever intended about the Indian, the key, the cupboard, and all the rest of it.

He and Patrick had talked about it, frantically, before his parents returned.

"How are you going to explain the burn on your head?" Patrick asked.

"I don't know. That's the one thing I can't explain."

"No, it's not. What about all the little bullet holes and stuff in your parents' bedroom?"

Omri's face was furrowed, even though every time he frowned, it hurt his burn.

"Maybe they won't notice. They both need glasses. Do you think we should clear everything up in there?"

Patrick had said, "No, better leave it. After all, they've got to know about the burglars. Maybe in all the fuss about *that,* they won't notice your face and a few other things."

"How shall we explain how we got rid of them—the burglars, I mean?"

"We could just say we burst in through the bathroom and scared them away."

Omri had grinned lopsidedly. "That makes us out to be heroes."

"So what's so bad about that? Anyway it's better than telling about *them.*" Patrick, who had once been quite keen to tell "about *them,*" now realized perfectly clearly that this was about the worst thing that could happen.

"But where *is* the wretched baby-sitter? Why didn't she come? How *dare* she not turn up when she *promised*?"

Omri's father was stamping up and down the living room in a fury. His mother, meanwhile, was holding Omri around the shoulders. He could feel her hand cold and shaking right through his shirt. After her first shocked outburst when she'd come home and seen him, she'd said very little. His father, on the other hand, couldn't seem to stop talking.

"You can't depend on anyone! Where the hell are the police? I called them hours ago!" (It was five minutes, in fact.) "One would think we lived on some remote island instead of in London, the biggest city in the world! You pay their salaries and when you need the police, they're never there, never!"

He paused in his pacing and gazed around wildly. The boys had put the television back and there wasn't much disorder in this room. Upstairs, they knew, chaos and endless unanswerable questions waited.

"Tell me again what happened."

"There were burglars, Dad," Omri said patiently. (This part was safe enough.) "Three of them. They came in through that window—"

"How many times have I said we ought to have locks fitted? Idiot that I am!—for the sake of a few lousy pounds— go on, go on—"

"Well, I was asleep in here—"

"In the living room? Why?"

"I—er—I just was. And I woke up and saw them, but they didn't see me. So I nipped upstairs and—"

His father, desperate to hear the story, was still too agitated to listen to more than a sentence of it without interrupting.

"And where were *you*, Patrick?"

Patrick glanced at Omri for guidance. Omri shrugged very slightly with his eyebrows. He didn't know himself how much to say and what to keep quiet about.

"I was—in Omri's room. Asleep."

"All right, all right! Then what?"

"Er—well, Omri came up, and woke me, and said there were burglars in the house, and that we ought to . . . er—" He stopped.

"Well?" barked Omri's father impatiently.

"Well . . . stop them."

Omri's father turned back to Omri. "Stop them? Three grown men? How could you stop them? You should have locked your bedroom door and let them get on with it!"

"They were nicking our TV and stuff!"

"So what? Don't you know the sort of people they are? They could have hurt you seriously—"

"They did hurt him seriously!" interrupted Omri's mother in a shrill voice. "Look at him! Never mind the interrogation now, Lionel. I wish you'd go and phone Basia and find out why she didn't come, and let me take Omri upstairs and look after him."

So Omri's father returned to the hall to phone the babysitter while his mother led Omri upstairs. But when she switched the bathroom light on and looked at him properly, she let out a gasp.

"But that's a burn, Omri! How—how did they do that to you?"

And Omri had to say, "They didn't do it, Mum. Not that. That was something else."

She stared at him in horror, and then controlled herself and said as calmly as she could, "All right, never mind now. Just sit down on the edge of the bath and let me deal with it."

And while she was putting on the ointment with her cold, shaky hands, his father came stamping up the stairs to say there was no reply from their baby-sitter's number.

"How could she not come?" he stormed. "How could she leave you boys alone here? Of all the criminally irresponsible—wait till I get hold of her—"

"What about us?" asked Omri's mother very quietly, winding a bandage around Omri's head.

"Us?"

"Us. Going out to our party before she got here."

"Well—well—but we trusted her! Thought she was just a few minutes late—" But his voice petered out, and he stopped stamping about and went into their bedroom to take off his coat.

Omri heard the light being switched on, and he bit his lips in suspense.

"Am I hurting, darling?"

He had no time to shake his head before his father burst back in.

"What in God's sweet name has been going on in our bedroom?"

Patrick, who was hanging about in the doorway to the bathroom, exchanged a grim look with Omri.

"Well, Dad—that's—that's where the battle—I mean, that's where they were, when we—caught them."

"Battle! That's just what it looks like, is a battlefield! Jane, come in here and look—"

Omri's mother left him sitting on the bath and went through into the bedroom. Omri and Patrick, numb and speechless with suspense, could hear them exchanging gasps and exclamations of amazement and dismay.

Then both his parents reappeared. Their faces had changed.

"Omri. Patrick . . . I think we'd better hear the whole story before the police arrive. Come in here."

With extreme reluctance, the boys went through the dividing door between bathroom and bedroom for the second time that evening.

The place looked terrible. All the dressing-table drawers, and those of the chest of drawers, were pulled out, their contents strewn about. The double bed had been knocked askew. A chair had gone flying, the wardrobe door was swinging open. Omri had set his mother's little jewel cupboard back on its feet, but its door, too, was open.

But with the lights full on, the thing the boys were most painfully aware of was the holes. Little pinholes made by the tiny bullets, and not so little ones made by the miniature mortars and hand grenades that had missed their targets and hit the wall and the head and foot of the bed. It seemed ludicrous to Omri now, looking at them, that he'd had even a faint hope his parents might not notice them. They might be a bit nearsighted, but after all, they weren't blind. The room looked pockmarked.

And indeed his father was already running his fingers over the white wall above the bed head.

"What's been going on here, boys?" he said in a new tone of voice.

Patrick and Omri glanced at each other, opened their mouths, and closed them again.

"Well?"

It wasn't a bark this time, it was just a question, a question filled with curiosity. After all, from a grown-up's point of view, what *could* make those tiny marks?

At that moment there was a loud, policemanly ring and double knock on the door.

Omri's father gave the boys a look that said, "This is only a short postponement," and left the room. They heard him running downstairs, and they all trailed after him. Halfway down, he paused.

"Good Lord, did you see this, Jane? I didn't notice as we came up! One of the banisters has been broken!"

Eager to explain something that could be explained, Omri volunteered the information that one of the burglars had fallen downstairs in his hurry to get out.

His father looked up at him.

"You boys must have thrown a real scare into them."

"Lionel," said Omri's mother suddenly.

"What?"

"Shouldn't we—hear what the boys have to say, before the police talk to them?"

He hesitated. The bell rang again, commandingly.

"Too late now," he said, and hurried to open the door to the police.

2.

Modest Heroes

As the two uniformed policemen were shown into the living room and Omri's mother hurried down to them, Omri and Patrick had a welcome moment to themselves at the top of the stairs.

"You look like a Sikh in that bandage," said Patrick. "Well, half a Sikh."

"Never mind what I look like. What are we going to do?"

Patrick said nothing for a moment. Then he said, "Make something up, I suppose. What else can we do?"

"All right. But what? What, that anyone'd believe for two seconds?"

"We might try saying that the skinheads did the damage to the wall. We could say they had—I don't know—spiked tools, gimlets or chisels or whatever, and just stuck them into everything for a laugh."

"Or we could say we don't know how they did it. We burst in, they ran, that's it. Leave the cops to figure it out."

"If they really look, they'll find minute bullets in the bottoms of the holes."

"They won't. Why should they think to?"

"Boys! Come down here, will you?"

It was Omri's dad calling, peremptorily. They started to walk as slowly as they dared down the stairs.

"And your burn?" whispered Patrick.

"Maybe—we might say we'd had a bonfire in the garden and that you cracked me over the head with a lighted branch."

"Oh, great! Try saying that and I really will crack you!"

So that was it. They didn't try to explain the little holes, and the police, assuming that the skinheads had been vandals as well as burglars, didn't examine them too closely. They went over everything else for fingerprints but said that although there were quite a few, the chances were against them catching the thieves who—technically speaking—weren't thieves after all, because they hadn't actually gotten away with anything.

Omri told the bonfire story without bringing Patrick into it. He just said—the inspiration of the moment—that they'd used a whole can of lighter fluid to get the fire going and that he, Omri, had struck the match while his face was over the wood. His parents, who had been positively bursting with pride at the way the boys had rid the house of intruders, abruptly changed their views about Omri's brilliance.

"How could you be so unutterably DAFT as to light a fire

like that, you little HALF-WIT!" his father expostulated. "How many times have I told you—"

A cough from one of the policemen interrupted him.

"Excuse me, sir. Were these two lads alone in the house?"

"Er—"

"Because as you no doubt know, sir, it is severely frowned on to leave any young person under the age of fourteen alone in a house at night."

"Of course I know that, Sergeant, and we never, never do it. We always have a baby-sitter. Very punctual and reliable. She was due at seven tonight, and when we went out we assumed she was a couple of minutes late. . . . She's never let us down before."

"And where is this person, sir?"

"She never showed up, Sergeant," said Omri's father shamefacedly. "Yes, I know what you're going to say, and you're perfectly right, we are to blame and I shall never forgive myself."

"I daresay you will, sir," said the sergeant levelly, "in time. But it would have been much harder to forgive yourself if *worse had befallen.*" Both Omri's parents hung their heads miserably, and Omri moved closer to his mother, who looked as if she might burst into tears.

"This is not exactly what you might call a—*salubrious* neighborhood, especially after dark," went on the policeman. "Only this evening a lady was mugged at the end of your street—pulled right off her bicycle, she was—"

"Her *bicycle!*"

This from Omri's mother, whose head had come up sharply.

"Yes, madam?"

"Who was she—this—lady who was mugged?"

The sergeant glanced at his companion. "Do you remember the name, George?"

George shrugged. "Some Polish-sounding name—"

Omri's mother and father exchanged horrified looks. "Not —was it Mrs. Brankovski?"

"Something like that—"

"But that's her! Our baby-sitter!" cried Omri's mother. "Oh, heavens—poor Basia—"

"Basha?" inquired the younger policeman. "Is that her name, or what happened to her—?" And he suppressed a snigger. But the sergeant gave him a stern look and he subsided.

"There's nothing humorous about it, George."

"No, Sergeant. Sorry."

"You'll be glad to hear she's not badly hurt, madam. But she had to go to the hospital, just for a checkup, like. The muggers got her bag, though."

"Oh, this is terrible! What kind of district have we come to live in?"

Ah, thought Omri. *Now maybe you'll realize what I've been going through, walking along Hovel Road to the station every day!* They'd never accepted before that it was a horrible area and that he'd been scared.

The policemen took all the details and descriptions of the skinheads.

"Could you identify them if you saw them again?" asked the sergeant.

"No," said Patrick.

Omri said nothing. He knew he would see them again, like on Monday morning on the way to school. Whether he would turn them in or not, he had yet to decide.

Adiel and Gillon came home from their film just as the police were leaving.

"And who are these young gentlemen?" asked the sergeant.

"They're Omri's older brothers."

"What's going on?" asked Adiel.

"We've had burglars," said Omri quickly.

"WHA-AT!" yelled Gillon. "They didn't get my stereo!— Did they?"

"They didn't get a thing," said their father proudly. "Omri and Patrick chased them off."

The older boys gaped at each other.

"Them and what army?" asked Gillon.

Patrick stifled a sudden nervous giggle. "Only a little one," he murmured. Omri nearly felled him with a heavy nudge.

There was a lot more talking to do—Adiel and Gillon had to hear the whole story (except that, of course, it was nothing like the whole story) all over again. They were absolutely agog, and even Gillon could find nothing sarcastic to say about the way Omri and Patrick had dealt with the situation.

"You're a pair of nutters," was the worst he could think of. "Those thugs could've flattened you. How did you know they didn't have knives?" But there was more than a hint of admiration in his reproof.

Adiel, the eldest, said, "Right pair of heroes if you ask me. We could've been cleaned out." And he gazed lovingly, not at his little brother, but at the television set.

It was nearly one o'clock in the morning by the time they'd drained the last of their hot chocolate and been gently shooed off to bed by Omri's mother. She gave Omri a special hug, being careful of his head, and hugged Patrick too.

"You're fantastic kids," she said.

Omri and Patrick looked uncomfortable. It simply didn't seem right to either of them that they were getting all the credit for driving off the intruders single- (or double-) handed, when in fact they'd had a great deal of help.

As soon as they got up to Omri's bedroom in the attic, they locked the door and made for the desk.

They'd had to make a hasty decision, before the return of the parents, to leave things as they were, not to send any-body else back after they'd dispatched Corporal Willy Fick-its and his men. As Patrick pointed out, "We don't know how the wounded would stand the journey. Besides, we can't send the Indians back to their time without Matron, we can't send *her* back to hers, without them—and we *certainly* can't send them all *anywhere* together!"

And Omri had agreed. But they'd both been on tenter-hooks all the time the police had been in the house for fear they'd demand to see Omri's room. The boys had been very careful to say the burglars hadn't got beyond the second floor of the house.

Now the boys bent over the desk. They'd left Omri's bed-side light on in case Matron had had to tend to one of the

wounded Indians in the night. She herself now sat, upright but clearly dozing, at a small circular table (made of the screw top of a Timotei shampoo bottle, a good shape because it had a rim she could get her knees under). On it lay a tiny clipboard which she had brought with her from St. Thomas's Hospital. She'd been making up her notes and temperature charts.

On either side of her on the floor of the longhouse stretched a double row of pallet beds. Each bed was occupied by a wounded Indian. Matron's ministrations had been so efficient that all were resting peacefully. She had earned her little nap, though she would probably deny hotly, later, that she had nodded off while "on duty."

Outside the longhouse, beside the burnt-out candle, a blanket was spread on the soil in Omri's father's seed tray. Curled up asleep on the blanket were Little Bear and Bright

Stars, his wife. Between them, in the crook of Bright Stars' arm, lay their newborn baby, Tall Bear.

All these people, when they were standing up, were no more than three inches tall.

3.

How It
All Started

It had all started more than a year before, with an old tin medicine cabinet Gillon had found, a key that fitted it, which had belonged to Omri's great-grandmother, and the little plastic figure of an American Indian that Patrick had given Omri (secondhand) for his birthday.

On that fateful night, Omri had put the Indian into the small metal cupboard and locked it with the fancy key. There was no particular point to this, really. Thinking back later, Omri didn't know why he'd done it. He'd had a thing at the time about secret cupboards, drawers, rooms; hiding places, kept safe from prying eyes, where he could secrete his favorite things and be sure they'd stay exactly as he'd left them, undisturbed by rummaging brothers or anyone else.

But the Indian didn't stay as he'd left it. Some combination of key and cupboard, plus the stuff the Indian was made of—plastic—had worked the wonder of bringing the little man to life.

At first, when this happened, Omri—once past the first shock of astonishment—had thought he was in for the fun trip of all time. A little, live man of his very own to play with! But it hadn't turned out like that.

The Indian, Little Bear, was no mere toy. Omri soon found out that he was a real person, somehow magicked into present-day London, England, from the America of nearly two hundred years ago. The son of a chief of the Iroquois tribe, a fighter, a hunter, with his own history and his own culture. His own beliefs and morals. His own brand of courage.

Little Bear regarded Omri as a magic being, a giant from the world of the spirits, and was at first terrified of him. Omri could see he was afraid, but the Indian was incredibly brave and controlled, and Omri soon began to admire him. He realized he couldn't treat him just as a toy—he was a person to be respected, despite his tiny size and relative helplessness.

And it soon turned out that he was by no means the easiest person in the world to get along with or satisfy. He had demands, and he made them freely, assuming Omri to be all-powerful.

He demanded his own kind of food. A longhouse, such as the Iroquois used to sleep in. A horse, although previously he had never ridden. Weapons, and animals to hunt, and a fire to cook on and dance around. Eventually he even demanded that Omri provide him with a wife!

In addition, Omri had to hide him and protect him. It needed only a little imagination to realize what would happen if any grown-up should find out about the cupboard, the key, and their magic properties. Because Omri soon found out that not just Little Bear but *any* plastic figure or object would become alive or real by being locked in the cupboard.

But he couldn't keep the secret entirely to himself. His best friend, Patrick, eventually found out about it and lost no time in putting his own little plastic man into the cupboard. And so "Boo-Hoo" Boone, the crying Texas cowboy, had come into their lives, complicating things still more. For of course, cowboy and Indian were enemies and had to be kept apart until a number of adventures, and their common plight—being tiny in a giants' world—brought them together and made them friends and even blood brothers.

Omri bought the plastic figure of an Indian girl and brought her to life as a wife for Little Bear. And shortly after that it was decided—with deep reluctance by the boys—that having three little people and their horses around amid all the dangers that threatened them in the boys' time and world, was more than they could cope with. It was just too much responsibility. So they "sent them back," for the cupboard and key worked also in reverse, transforming real miniature people back into plastic and returning them to their own time.

Omri hadn't intended ever to play with this dangerous magic again. It had been too frightening, too full of problems—and too hurtful, at the end, when he had to part with friends he had grown so fond of. But as with so many resolutions, this one got broken.

About a year later, by which time Omri's and Patrick's

families had both moved, Omri won a prize in an important competition for a short story. The story he wrote was called "The Plastic Indian" and was all about—well, it was the truth, but of course no one thought of that; they just thought Omri had made up the most marvelous tale. And he was so excited (the prize was three hundred pounds, he was to receive it at a big party in a London hotel, and even his brothers were impressed) that he decided to bring Little Bear back to life, just long enough to share this triumph with him since he had been such a vital part of it.

Unfortunately, things were not so simple.

When Omri put Little Bear, Bright Stars, and their pony —the plastic figures of them—back in the cupboard, they emerged much changed.

Little Bear lay across the back of his pony with two musket balls in his back, very near death. There had been a battle in his village, between his tribe and their enemies, the Algonquins, together with French soldiers (Omri had already learned that the French and English had been fighting in America at the time, and Little Bear's tribe was on the English side). Little Bear had been wounded. Bright Stars, although on the point of having a baby, had rushed out and heaved Little Bear onto his pony, just as the magic worked, bringing them—tiny as before, but as real as ever, and in desperate trouble—to Omri's attic bedroom.

And thus it was that Omri was launched into a whole series of new and even more hair-raising and challenging adventures.

Luckily Patrick was nearby and was able to help with some excellent ideas. Boone "came back" too, and they also brought to life a hospital Matron from a much more recent era to help save Little Bear's life. Later, when he demanded to go back to his village, a British Royal Marine corporal, Willy Fickits, and a contingent of Iroquois braves were brought to life to help take revenge on the Algonquins.

At this point there was a most incredible turn of events.

Boone, the cowboy, suggested that the boys go back to Little Bear's time and witness the battle. Of course they thought it was impossible. How could they fit into the little bathroom cupboard, only about a foot high? But Boone pointed out that the magic key might fit something larger— the old seaman's chest that Omri had bought in the market, for instance.

It worked. Each boy climbed in in turn, the other one turned the key, and each separately went back in time to the Iroquois village.

When Omri got back—terribly shaken after witnessing a

horrific battle—his hair was singed and he had a burn blister on the side of his head.

The boys brought the Indian troop back through the magic of the key, discovering to their horror that the modern weapons that they had given Little Bear's men—Little Bear called them now-guns—had proved too much for fighters accustomed to bows and arrows. Many of them had been accidentally shot by their own side. Matron had to be brought back to treat their wounds, but eight had been killed.

Little Bear was distraught, but Bright Stars comforted him by putting his new son, Tall Bear, in his arms. And Omri and Patrick took the blame. They shouldn't have sent modern weapons into the past. . . . But these worked very well when, later, three skinheads tried to burgle the house. The boys brought some plastic Marines to life and mounted an artillery assault on them just as they were rifling Omri's parents' bedroom, and completely routed them. It was exhilarating while it lasted, but now they were faced with the aftermath: reality, the present, the results of the night's doings.

4.

Dead
In The Night

The two boys sat on the floor of Omri's bedroom and conferred in low voices.

"We've got to plan what to do," said Patrick. "One of us must be up here in your room, on guard, every minute of the rest of the weekend. We'll have to keep your door locked from inside. Whoever's not here will have to bring food and stuff, so I'd better stay up here most of the time. It'll look dead odd if *I* start nicking stuff from your kitchen. I don't know what we're going to do on Monday—"

Omri said heavily, "I do. I'll have to go to school, and you'll have to go home."

"Oh, God, yes," said Patrick, remembering.

Patrick now lived in Kent with his mother. They were in London only for a brief visit to his aunt and girl cousins, Emma and the dreadful Tamsin. They'd have been back in their country home already if Tamsin had not fallen off her bicycle and hurt herself, so that Patrick's mother had decided to stay on for a day or two to help his aunt.

The boys sat in heavy silence. Omri could hardly bear the thought of being left alone in this increasingly difficult situation. Patrick could hardly bear the thought of leaving it.

"Maybe Tamsin'll die," Patrick said darkly. "Then we'll have to stay on. For the funeral."

Omri hoped this was only a sick joke. He detested Tamsin, but he didn't wish her dead—not now that he'd seen death, not with those eight small bloodstained bodies lying under torn-up scraps of sheet, right here in his room.

"What are we going to do about—the casualties?" he asked.

"You mean the dead ones? We'll have to bury them."

"Where?"

"In your garden?"

"But we can't just . . . I mean, it's not like when Boone's horse died. They're people, we can't just—stick them in the earth. What about their families?"

"Their families are—are *back there* somewhere. We don't know where they are or *when* they are."

"Maybe we ought to—to send them back through the cupboard, to their own time."

"Send their dead bodies back? With modern bullets in them?"

"Their people would think they'd been shot by white men. They wouldn't examine them. They'd go through—you know, whatever special rituals they have, and bury them properly—or—or whatever they do with dead people."

Abruptly Omri felt his eyes begin to prick, and a hard, hot lump came into his throat. He put his head down on his knees. Patrick must have been feeling the same, because he squeezed Omri's arm sympathetically.

"It's no good feeling it too much," he said after clearing his throat twice. "I know it's terrible and I know it's partly our fault. But they lived in very dangerous times, fighting and risking death every day. And they went into the battle quite willingly."

"They didn't know what they were up against with the now-guns," said Omri in a muffled voice.

"Yeah, I know. Still. It doesn't help to—to be a Boone."

The weak joke about the crybaby cowboy made Omri chuckle just a little.

"Where is Boone, by the way?" he asked, sniffing back his tears.

"I told you. I sent him back—he asked me to. Gave him a new horse, and off he went. Look."

He opened the cupboard. On the shelf was Boone, standing beside his new horse, a tall, alert-looking black one. On the floor of the cupboard, Corporal Fickits and his men were clustered together, with their various weapons. Patrick gathered them all up, put the soldiers back in the biscuit tin, but kept Fickits and Boone separate. Boone went into his pocket, horse and all. He always kept him there, when he wasn't real, for luck. He was actually as fond of Boone as Omri was of Little Bear. Omri put Fickits in the back pocket of his jeans.

"The only thing we can do right now is to get some sleep," Omri said.

Patrick settled down on his floor cushions while Omri

clambered up onto his bunk bed under the skylight. He looked up at the stars through the branches of the old elm tree which his father kept saying should be cut down because it was dead. Skeletal as it was, to Omri it was a friend.

"Let's bring Boone back tomorrow," Patrick whispered just before they dropped off. "I don't seem to be able to face things without Boone, whether he cries or not. Besides, I want to know if he likes his new horse."

At dawn Omri was awakened by a familiar shout.

"Omri, wake! Day come! Much need do!"

Omri, feeling sticky-eyed and thick-headed with tiredness, slid backwards down the ladder to the floor. Patrick was still sound asleep. The gray dawn light was just creeping through the skylight.

"It's dead early, Little Bear," he muttered, rubbing his face and stifling a series of yawns.

Little Bear didn't hear him properly. He caught only his name and the word "dead." He nodded his hard-muscled face once and grunted.

"One more dead in night."

Omri's throat closed up with a sick feeling.

"Another? Oh, no . . . I'm sorry!" He meant sorry-ashamed, not just sorry-regretful. He felt every dead Indian brave was on his own conscience. He should never have made the modern weapons real, never have sent Little Bear and his braves back in time with them. The trouble was, he seemed *still* not fully to have accepted the fact, which he knew with one part of his brain, that these little people were not just toys come to life. They were flesh and blood, with their own characters, their own lives and destinies. And against his own intentions Omri had been drawn in. He'd found himself acting out his own part in these destinies, which would never have been possible but for the magic of the cupboard . . . and the key.

The key turned any container into a kind of body-shrinking time machine. His seaman's chest had taken him and Patrick back to the eighteenth century, to Little Bear's time and place. Omri had not had time, so far, even to begin to think about the possibilities of that.

Now he scanned the seed tray and saw that two of the Indians who had not been injured were carrying another body out of the longhouse and into the little paddock Patrick had made with miniature fencing for the ponies, and which was now a makeshift morgue. Matron followed the sad procession, her face, rather grim at all times, now grimmer than ever.

"I did my best," she said shortly. "Bullet lodged in the liver. Couldn't reach it."

She watched the two braves lay the dead Indian down beside the others. Suddenly she turned to face Omri.

"I know I did that operation on your friend!" she said. "And I operated last night—emergency ops—three of them —but blow it all, I'm not a surgeon! Stupid of me—*conceited* —to think I could cope. Can't. Not trained for it. Anyway . . . too much for any one person." Her voice cracked.

"Matron, it's not your fault—" began Omri, terrified that this capable, efficient, down-to-earth woman might be about to burst into tears, which would have unmanned him completely.

"Didn't say it was! My fault indeed!" She glared at him,

took her spectacles off, polished them on a spotless handkerchief from her apron pocket, and put them back on her formidable nose.

"Blessed if I know how I got here, what this is all about. Now don't you go pulling the wool over my eyes, I know when I'm dreaming and when I'm not—this is *real.* The blood's real, the pain's real, the deaths are real. My ops were real, they were the best I could do, but what is also real is my —my—my basic *inadequacy.*"

She suddenly snatched the handkerchief out of her pocket again and blew her nose on it. She wiped her nose back and forth several times and then gave a great, convulsive sniff.

"What we need here is a properly equipped medical team!"

Omri gaped at her.

"If we don't get one—and quickly—more of these poor men are going to die."

After a moment, during which she glared at him expectantly through her spectacles, Omri said slowly, "I'll tell you the truth about your being here and—all the rest of it. But you probably won't believe me."

"After what I've been through in the past forty-eight hours, I'll believe anything!" she said fervently.

He explained things as well as he could. She listened intently and asked a couple of questions.

"You say any article or figure made of plastic is affected?"

"Yes."

"And objects that might be concealed on the person—my hypodermic syringe, for example, and other things I brought in my pocket from St. Thomas's—"

"Yes, they're made real, provided the person had them on him before he was—*brought.*"

"Well! Why can't you get hold of some plastic doctors and put them in your allegedly magic cupboard? Only you must make sure they have some equipment—surgical instruments and so forth."

"But all the shops are shut! How can I—"

Suddenly Omri remembered. Two nights ago he had gone to see Patrick at his aunt's house, and they had tried to borrow Tamsin's new box of plastic figures, only she'd caught them at it and grabbed it back. Omri had just managed to hold onto the figure that turned out to be Matron. But there had been others in the set—including a surgeon at an operating table.

He stretched out his foot and nudged Patrick awake.

"Patrick! Listen. There's another Indian dead. And Matron says, if we don't find a proper doctor, more will die."

Patrick scrambled to his feet, rubbing his hair.

"How can we get any new ones on Sunday?"

"What about the ones Tamsin has?"

"What are you saying? That I should go back to Auntie's and nick them when Tamsin isn't looking?"

"It's only borrowing."

"Not when the owner doesn't know or agree! Not when the owner's my little creep of a cousin! She'd have my guts for garters."

Omri said with a note of desperation, "Well, what *are* we going to do, then? This is a real emergency!" Suddenly he had an idea. "Why don't you try buying them off her?"

"It might work. Have you got any dosh?"

"Not a penny, we spent it all on the Indian braves. Maybe Dad'll lend me a couple of quid."

Omri's Dad did better than that. He gave him five pounds, and not just till pay day. "You've earned it. Here's one for Patrick, too."

So there was no problem about money.

At breakfast, hastily eaten, the boys sneaked some crispy bits of bacon and quite a few Crunchy Nutflakes into their pockets, and Omri astonished his mother by asking for a mug of tea instead of milk. Matron couldn't cope without her tea.

"I thought you hated tea!"

"I'm coming around to it."

"You'll be hitting the scotch next," commented his father from behind his Sunday paper.

Patrick nudged Omri. When whisky was mentioned, there was just one person who came to mind. Halfway back up the stairs, Patrick whispered, "Let's bring Boone back to life right now, before I leave!"

At that moment the doorbell rang.

Omri went back down and opened the door. Then he gasped. Outside stood Tamsin. Of all people!

How could it be? She'd broken her leg!

Omri looked again. It wasn't Tamsin, it was Emma.

Emma was Tamsin's twin sister. She was the spitting image of Tamsin, and yet she was wholly different. As far as Omri could remember, she was quite a decent sort of girl.

"Hallo, Omri," she said. "Can I see Patrick?"

Patrick dragged himself reluctantly down into the hall. Omri stood aside, waiting. He could feel himself tensing all over for fear there was a car outside waiting to cart Patrick away.

"Hi, Em. How's it going?" said Patrick carelessly.

"Okay. Tam's leg's in a cast and she's better. They sent me here because Omri's phone's busted and your mum couldn't ring you and you're to come back with me."

"Right *now?*"

"Yes."

"I—I can't come now!"

"Why not?"

Patrick dithered helplessly, trying to think of some excuse.

"How are we supposed to get back?"

"On the train, of course," said Emma. "Come on."

Omri said, "Did *you* come here on the train?"

"Yes, why?"

"And you walked up the road to here, from the station?"

"Yes."

Omri thought of the skinheads. It was Sunday—even the few who went to school or had jobs were free and on the prowl on Sundays. He himself never walked down Hovel Road on Sundays if he could possibly help it.

"Did you meet anyone?"

She shrugged. "A few boys. Hanging around. Real creeps, *gross.* I took no notice of them."

Omri shivered. But then he remembered. There was a pretty good chance he didn't have to be scared of that gang anymore. He put his hand in his jeans pocket and fingered the little penlight the smallest of the burglars had dropped the night before.

As he touched it, he felt something else. It was the key. A

sudden flash of inspiration came to him, stiffening his whole body like a bolt of electricity.

"Emma," he said in a queer sort of voice, "would you mind if I had a private chat with Patrick before he—er—goes?"

She looked from one of them to the other. "What's the secret?"

They both flushed.

"Wait here, okay?" Omri gabbled, and he pulled Patrick into the living room and closed the door.

"You've *got* to get out of going home," Omri said. "I can't cope without you."

"What can I do? Break *my* leg?"

"Well . . . if you had the bottle for it, you could throw yourself down the stairs . . . probably do yourself *some* serious enough injury—"

"Thanks!"

"But I wasn't thinking of that. Tell Emma you've left something upstairs. We'll go up to my room and you can get in the chest with Boone's figure and I can send you back to his time."

5.

Patrick
Goes Back

Patrick's face was blank for a moment, and Omri thought, *He's scared, and who can blame him!* But then he saw it wasn't that at all. Patrick simply hadn't been able to grasp the idea at first.

When he did grasp it, not just his face but his whole body seemed to light up with excitement.

"Wow," he said simply.

"You mean you'll do it?"

"Are you kidding? Go back to real cowboy time, cowboy country? See Boone full-size? Lead me to it! Let's go!"

He bounded out of the living room and was halfway up the stairs before Omri had gathered his wits to follow. As he came into the hall, he noticed Emma standing much closer to the living room door than she had been before. Patrick had nearly bowled her over as he emerged.

A suspicion struck Omri.

"Were you listening?"

"Yes," she said at once. "But I didn't understand what you were talking about."

"Ah," said Omri with relief. It crossed his mind that she was a very straightforward girl, at least—Tamsin wouldn't have admitted eavesdropping like that. Not many people would.

He gave Emma a closer look. She was a year younger than he was—which was why he had hardly noticed her at school; somehow you only noticed your contemporaries or people ahead of you. But she'd been more or less around for most of his life. Odd that he'd never really looked at her before. Now he saw that she was quite nice looking in a fair, snubby-faced way. She had freckles and large eyes, and was dressed in sensible jeans and a blue parka. She had her hands deep in her pockets and was gazing at him expectantly.

"What *were* you talking about in there?"

"Private," said Omri. He glanced up the stairs. Patrick could already be heard thudding up the last flight, to Omri's attic bedroom.

"Where's Patrick gone?"

"Er—up to get his pajamas and stuff."

"But he didn't take any last night, he just dashed out."

"Oh. Well—anyway he's—gone up," said Omri feebly, making a move to follow him.

Emma followed at his heels. He paused on the second step.

"Can you wait down here?"

"Why?"

"We'll be—right down."

"Can't I see your room? You saw mine," she said. "Last night when you came to our house. Mum moved Tam and me out so Patrick could have it."

"Well . . ."

From above came Patrick's impatient voice. "Come *on*, Omri! Don't hang about!"

"You wait in the living room," Omri said decisively. He turned away from her and ran upstairs.

In his room he found Patrick already climbing into the seaman's chest.

"Go on, I'm ready! Send me!"

But Omri, having come up with this amazing idea, was already having second thoughts.

"Listen, how'll I explain where you've gone?"

"Don't. Get rid of Emma somehow, make her go home, and you can tell your parents I went with her."

"But what happens when Emma gets back to her place without you?"

"It'll be too late then! I'll just have vanished!" He grinned all over his face with glee.

"No, you won't. You'll be in the chest—your body will. What if they start looking for you?"

"Listen, this was your idea, and a fantastic one! Stop making problems. Pile all your junk on top of the chest like before—they'll never think to look there."

"But your mum will be dead worried! She's sure to ring up. Then Emma will say one thing and I'll say another—"

Patrick had been crouching in the chest, looking up at him. Now, suddenly, he stood up. His face had changed. He looked quite fierce.

"I want to go back with Boone," he said. "I've made up my

mind. And I don't want you bringing me back after ten minutes, either. You had your adventure in the Indian village. I know you had a rough time, but you *saw* it, you saw the battle, you *experienced* it. Now it's my turn, and I don't want to hear any of your feeble objections. Just put the key in the lock and turn it, will you? I'm the one who's taking the risk. All you're asked to do is stall everybody for a few days."

Omri's mouth dropped open.

"A few *days?*"

"It's hardly worth going for less than that!" Patrick retorted.

That he would stay away for longer than a few hours had not been any part of Omri's—as he now saw it—idiotic idea.

"But it could be dangerous! What if—"

Patrick made a move as if to get out of the chest. "Are you going to do it, or am I going to have to bash you?" he growled.

Omri was not afraid of him. They were evenly matched. He stood his ground.

"You don't have to use skinhead tactics," he said.

Patrick looked sheepish.

"Sorry. You're always trying to hold me back from doing what I want to. Listen. We'd better decide beforehand when you're going to bring me back. Time works the same at both ends. So let's say—a week from today."

"You're completely round the twist," said Omri. "A week! Anyone'd think you were going on holiday! All right, lie down. I'll send you. But don't get too comfortable in Texas, because you'll be back before you know it, if I get into any trouble about you, which I'm bound to."

Patrick stared at him for a moment, then slowly took the

small figure of Boone out of his pocket. Omri reached out and touched it. He wanted to touch Patrick—shake hands with him or something—but he didn't know how to do it, quite. So he touched Boone instead and said, "Say hello to him for me and tell him—tell him to take good care of you."

Patrick curled up in the bottom of the chest. Omri, feeling quite calm now that the decision was made, closed the lid. He took the key out of his pocket and stuck it in the lock on the chest. For a moment it hung there, its red satin ribbon hanging from its fancy top. Then Omri turned it firmly.

At that moment he heard a small, shrill voice nearby.

"What Pat-Rick do? Why move longhouse? Very bad, move sick men, make fear, make wound worse!"

Omri spun around. In order to open the chest, Patrick had lifted the seed tray with its precious miniature complement of Indians, healthy, injured, and dead, on to Omri's desk underneath his raised bunk bed. Omri had, for the moment, quite forgotten them. Now he saw Little Bear standing at the edge of the tray, his arms folded, and his face, lit by Omri's desk lamp, a mask of reproach.

"What Pat-Rick do in box?"

Omri crouched till his face was level with Little Bear's.

"Little Bear, Patrick's gone. We agreed he should go back to Boone's time. He's going to stay there for a while. So if there's anything you need, you'll have to ask me."

"I ask, you not fear," said Little Bear promptly.

Omri suppressed a sigh. There wouldn't be much of the "ask" about it, if he knew Little Bear.

"Start with food. Wife must feed son. Need good food, keep up strength."

"Oh—of course! Sorry, I almost forgot."

Omri reached into his pocket and brought out his collection of cornflakes, bits of bacon and toast, which he'd thoughtfully wrapped in a paper napkin. Of course he'd left the mug of tea downstairs. He'd have to go and get it. Meanwhile there was enough food to be getting on with for all of them.

Little Bear looked at the spread, sampled a chunk of crispy bacon fat, and grunted with grudging approval. But then he straightened up, his face once more a mask of seriousness.

"Not leave dead brave long time," Little Bear said. "Send back. Own people find, know what do, obey custom for dead."

"Yes," said Omri. "That's what we thought. When?"

"Ry-taway," said Little Bear, who was beginning to pick up some English expressions.

"We'll put them in the cupboard," said Omri. He felt the cupboard was the right time vehicle for the little people, the chest for him and Patrick.

The logistics of the thing were solved by Omri's putting his left hand palm upward on the soil in the seed tray while Little Bear and three healthy Indians carefully and reverently lifted the corpses, still covered with bloodstained cloths, onto it. Omri shuddered as he felt their body weight, the coldness of death against his skin. Then the "burial party" of four climbed onto Omri's hand and he slowly moved to the cupboard, which stood on the low table in the middle of his room.

He opened the door. Two Indians climbed off his hand and over the bottom edge of the cupboard, and the other two lifted the bodies one by one and handed them to the

Indians, who then laid them on the floor of the metal cupboard.

Omri reached over and took the key from the lock of the
chest and inserted it into the keyhole of the cupboard. The
"burial party" climbed out and stood in a line, looking at
their dead comrades in silence.

"Little Bear," said Omri, "what about if you all go back
now? There's nothing to hang around here for, and there's a
lot to do, rebuilding your village. I'm sure Bright Stars would
like to take the baby back and get on with her life."

Little Bear turned to him, scowling with thought.

"Good," he said. "Go back soon ry-taway. First you send
dead, then take out plass-tick."

Omri closed the door, turned the key, and after a moment
turned it back, opened the door, and removed the nine
plastic figures. He knew they were no use anymore—the
people belonging to them were gone. He certainly wouldn't
ever want to play with them. After a second's thought, he

took a piece of white writing paper and, piling them onto it, folded the edges carefully around them.

"I'll bury them," he said to Little Bear. "That's our custom with dead people."

Little Bear nodded grimly. "Good. First we do dance, ask Great Spirit bring safe to ancestors."

Matron had come out of the longhouse, serving as a sort of field hospital for the injured Indians, and watched the removal of the dead. Now she called Omri over.

"I'm very much relieved that you've dealt with that matter," she said in her brisk way. "Now. Having disposed of the dead, do you think you could give your urgent attention to the problem of those who are still alive?"

Omri felt a little jolt in his chest. Now that Patrick had abandoned him, he must solve by himself the pressing problem of getting the medical team.

"Matron, look," he said, thinking aloud more than anything else, "it's Sunday. Can't go to the shops. We . . . that is, I thought I'd try to get some help from a friend who has plastic figures. Not exactly a friend. She's Patrick's cousin—"

"Who, me?"

The jolt Omri had felt before was nothing to the explosive leap his heart gave at the sound of that voice.

He spun around from his ill-balanced crouch, falling over backwards, and sat gaping at the figure of Emma in the open doorway.

6.

A New Insider

"Emma! What—what—what are you doing there?"

But it was only too obvious what she was doing. She was looking. And listening. The only question left was, how much had she seen and heard?

In a forlorn and desperate hope, Omri swiveled his eyes sideways, trying to see what was visible from her angle. Before, when he'd been crouching in front of the desk, he had blocked her view of the seed tray. Now that he was on the floor, everything was in plain sight. Matron's little figure, standing, arms akimbo, on the edge of the seed tray. Little Bear's pony, grazing in the miniature paddock Patrick had made. Several tiny Indians, busy about the area, rebuilding last night's fire from the unburned ends of matchsticks and twigs. And the longhouse, rising from the ground in all its minute, handmade magnificence.

But Emma was not looking as far as that. On the low table that stood between her and Omri was the cupboard, and the five Indians. They were chanting and doing a slow dance around the white paper packet. It was upon them, Omri saw, that Emma's eyes were riveted.

There was nothing to be done. Naught. Zilch. Zipadee-doo-dah. Zero. *And when that's the case,* thought Omri in a sudden mood of fatalism, *you might as well relax.*

"Well," he said, his voice coming out quite steady, "what do you think?"

She stared at them for a long time, her eyes fixed and unblinking, her freckles standing out on a suddenly very pale face.

"They're alive," she said at last, in a doubtful tone, as if he might roar with laughter at her.

"You don't say," said Omri, scrambling to his feet. "And not only those. What about these, here?" And he indicated the seed tray behind him.

Emma moved cautiously forward, as if afraid the very floor might waver and give way beneath her feet. He noticed now that she had a mug of tea in her hand, the one he'd saved from breakfast—it must have been the excuse she'd given herself for following him up. It tilted in her nerveless fingers, and he removed it to safety.

As he poured a few drops into a toothpaste cap for Matron, Omri watched Emma as she gazed and gazed. He knew that what his father called a quantum leap had been taken in the situation, the sort of change that means nothing will be quite

the same again, and that was scary. But there was no deny-
ing a sort of enjoyment in watching someone else seeing,
trying to realize, coming to grips with it.

Emma managed this last feat surprisingly quickly.

"I've always thought it could happen," she said abruptly.
"It often nearly has, when I've been playing with my toy
animals. Can they talk? Oh, of course they can, that's who
you were talking to."

Matron's voice, little but scratchy as chalk on a black-
board, chirped up. "And pray who might this young person
be? I don't believe we've been introduced."

Emma turned a suddenly flushed and smiling face on
Omri. "Wow! Omri, what fun! How fantastic! I mean, how
brill can anything get!"

"Yeah," said Omri somewhat sourly. "Brill. Except that in
that little hut there are some men who are wounded and
who could die if we don't do something. And they're real,
and I'm responsible for them, and Patrick's P.O.'d—"

"P.O.'d, what's that?"

"Er—gone. And—"

"Gone? Where?"

Omri took a deep breath. "There's no time to explain everything now. Listen. You know that set of plastic figures Tamsin got for her birthday?"

Emma was one jump ahead of him. Her face lit up another few watts. "Yes! Yes! I got one too! You mean we can make them all come alive—be real, like these?"

Omri grabbed her arm. "Wait, did you say you got the same set of models as Tamsin?"

She shook off his hand. "Don't pinch! No, mine was different, mine was a sort of shop with people with trolleys and checkouts and—"

Omri's heart sank. "Not doctors?"

She shook her head. "No. I wanted the doctors and all that, but Tam wouldn't swap."

Omri said, "Would she *sell* hers?"

"Got the odd hundred quid, have you?" said Emma cynically.

"I've got the odd *five* quid."

Emma frowned, considering. "She might not be able to resist. She's saving for a skiing holiday."

"Patrick's got another fiver," said Omri. "I could—" He turned automatically toward the chest. Then stopped.

"Er . . . listen, Em. I'm prepared to let you in on most of this—well, you are in on it. But there're a couple of wrinkles I think you might not . . . exactly feel comfortable about, not just at first. So would you mind going downstairs for a few minutes? Then I'm going back to your place with you, and we'll negotiate for the models with Tam."

She hesitated. "And then come back here and—do whatever it is you do to make them come alive?"

Omri looked at her. Now she knew about the little people. But she didn't yet know about the magic, how to make it happen. She didn't really know much, when you came right down to it. There wasn't a lot she could give away. Not that anyone would believe. And that was the nitty-gritty, not her knowing, but her maybe telling. Could he trust her? Could one trust *anyone* with a secret as exciting as this?

"We'll have to have a serious talk," he said. "On the train. Just now I want you to go out. Please, Em."

They looked at each other. He actually saw her decide to give way, whether to please him or for reasons of her own he wasn't sure. It didn't matter anyhow. Just so she went.

The second she was outside he shot the bolt, to make sure. Then he rushed to the cupboard, took the key out, stuck it back in the chest, and turned it.

Patrick lay curled up as Omri had seen him once before,

and he remembered his thought that other time: *As far away as you can get without being dead.* It was tempting to stand there, losing himself in speculation about where the real Patrick was.

But there was no time for such thoughts. Reaching into the chest, Omri fumbled in Patrick's pocket for the five-pound note. And touched something that made him snatch his hand away with a yelp as if he'd burned it.

There was something alive in Patrick's pocket!

Omri stood there with his heart in his gullet. It wasn't a person; it was a tiny animal of some kind. With his fingertips Omri had felt that much. Patrick must have had something plastic in his pocket when he was locked in the chest, and it had come to life!

Cautiously Omri stuck his fingers into the pocket again. Yes, there it was, something small, smooth-coated and bony.

He took hold of it as gently as he could, feeling it struggle and twist. He drew it out.

It was a very distressed black horse, complete with an old Western-style saddle and bridle.

Boone's horse! His new one, that Patrick had taken from the English soldier. Omri set it down very gently in the paddock on the seed tray, where Little Bear's pony was tethered with a double-ply nylon thread. It threw up its head as the intruder descended from the heavens, and whinnied anxiously, but as soon as the black pony's feet were on the ground and it had given itself a good shake, both their heads dropped to graze the turf of real grass Patrick had dug up and laid there.

Omri smiled in relief. Evidently Boone's pony was all right, though he wished he could take off its bridle and saddle. Boone must have put his old tack on it before Patrick had sent him back—

Suddenly Omri went rigid, his brain fizzing with the shock of the realization that had come to him.

But how could they have been so stupid!

In all the haste and hassle of getting Patrick "sent back," they'd forgotten! Forgotten the way it worked! Patrick had had the *plastic figure* of Boone in his hand, not the real, live Boone! That meant—

That meant that Boone, like the horse, would have become real inside the chest!

"Boone!" he called frantically into the depths of the chest. "Boone! Where are you? Are you okay?"

Silence.

Omri grabbed Patrick's right arm. His hand was tucked under his body. Omri dragged it out from under Patrick's dead weight. The fingers were closed into a tight fist. Sticking out from the top of it was a tuft of ginger hair.

Grimly, desperately, Omri prised Patrick's fingers open.

In his hand lay Boone, the real Boone. Limp. Motionless.

Dead?

Crushed?

"Matron!"

Before she knew it, that stalwart lady had been snatched off the seed tray and set down, somewhat short of breath and dignity, on the low table.

"Not another patient! I've got more than I can—" Then she saw. Her voice changed. "Oh dear me," she said softly. "Oh, dearie, dearie me."

With a doomful look, she fell to her knees beside the supine figure of Boone and applied her ear to his heart. To his horror, Omri saw her give her head half a shake.

7.

Patrick
In Boone-Land

Patrick's journey through time and space was swift and painless. There was a strange sort of *whooosh* during which he seemed to feel, for a split second, buffeted, as when two heavy trucks pass close by each other traveling at high speed in opposite directions. Then there was heat, silence, and stillness.

He opened his eyes to the glare of a harsh sun and screwed them shut.

He felt around with his hands. There seemed to be nothing directly in front of him. But he felt he was upright and leaning against something blanket-like, but stiffer, rather like a wall covered with flannel.

Then he found that there was something like a wide, thick cord across his middle, holding him against the soft wall. He opened his eyes cautiously. At first he couldn't see anything but glaring sunlight. But in a few moments he got accustomed to that and found himself staring out across an endless expanse of sand.

"Well," he said aloud, "it's Texas, I suppose, so this must be a bit of desert or prairie or something."

But where was he? Where—in all this sand—*was* he?

He looked downward. His hands were resting on a thick rope-like thing as thick as his own leg, stretched quite tightly across his waist. Under his feet was something that curved away on either side of him and curled up several yards ahead of him. It was like standing on the brink of a huge, smooth, pale-brown—and empty—riverbed. Behind him it rose up like the bank of the river, but the bank felt soft to his hand, and suddenly he realized what it was.

"It's—it's a gigantic *hat!*" he said aloud. "I'm tied to the crown of it, and this thing must be the hatband, only it's a huge leather cord!"

He wriggled down until he was free of the cord, into which he seemed to have been stuck quite casually like a feather, or like the flies that fishermen sometimes stick in their hatbands. Suddenly Patrick remembered that Boone had had some kind of a tiny favor—so small one could hardly see it, except that it was blue, like his own jeans and sweatshirt—in the cord around his much-loved cowboy hat.

Patrick crawled rapidly across the width of the brim toward its curled-up edge.

As he did so he noticed for the first time the utter silence around him, and the fact that the hat was perfectly still.

I must be on Boone's head, he thought. *Why isn't the hat jiggling about as he rides?*

He reached the edge of the brim, pulled himself up to it,

and peered over, preparing himself to see an immense drop below.

The sand lay no more than four or five times Patrick's own height beneath him.

He could easily make out the individual grains, which looked to him like the shingle on an English beach, except that some of them were like lumps of yellow glass.

Suddenly he stiffened and gasped. A huge creature, about the size of a Galápagos tortoise, moseyed by on six angled legs. Patrick shrank back behind the rim of the hat; then, realizing that it was merely some kind of beetle and that it couldn't reach him, he raised himself cautiously and followed its progress off across the endless expanse of sand.

He looked around, as far as he could for the enormous bulk of the hat, which loomed against the sky like a soft-cornered building. There was no sign of anything else alive.

The first thing is to get down from here, he thought. *Even if it's dangerous. There's no point in staying here.*

He considered the problem of getting down to the ground. If the sand below had been his size of sand, he might have risked jumping into it (or then again, he thought, peering down, he might not!). But it would be suicide to jump down onto those big, hard stones. He'd have to lower himself somehow.

Patrick, unlike Omri, was athletic. He really shone in PE, and loved climbing and jumping and swinging. What he needed now was some kind of rope, and of course the first thing he thought of was the hatband.

He followed it around the crown of the hat again until he found the knot. Luckily, it was old; the leather itself was soft, and the knot loosely tied. By forcing one of the ends back upon itself through the knot, twice, he managed to untie it. Then, with great effort, he managed to drag one end around the crown until he had about half of it at his disposal, and he carefully lowered the free end down over the brim.

The immediate danger was that his weight, though relatively slight, would pull the whole thong to the ground when he tried to slide down it, but he had to risk that. Taking a deep breath, he threw his right leg over the stiff brim, embraced the thong with arms and legs as if he were sliding down a tree trunk, and away he went.

He was down almost before he had time to think, and as his feet touched the stones, he felt the rest of the thong fall away from the hat. He just managed to leap aside as it fell, like an immense and heavy snake, onto the ground, missing him by a hair's breadth.

He took another deep breath and looked around.

The first thing he saw was a huge, impenetrable mass of what looked like fine copper fuse wires.

He touched one. It was very flexible—it certainly wasn't a wire. It was more like—

Patrick gasped. He suddenly knew what it was. And, knowing that, he knew in a flash that something had gone very wrong.

The mass of wires was Boone's ginger hair, sticking out from underneath his hat.

Patrick started to run. It was not easy, running on the glassy shingle, but, trying not to stumble too often, he made his way as fast as he could right around to the other side of the huge thing like a promontory—which was actually Boone's head—jutting out of the desert landscape.

When he got there, he stopped, stared, stepped back,

stared again. At last he realized that to get the face in perspective he would have to move back still farther. He turned and ran away from it for about a hundred paces, then turned again.

Yes. Now he could see it was Boone.

He was lying on his side, the bulk of him rising from the flat desert floor like a range of hills. Though his face was turned to the side, the hat was lying horizontally across one ear as if someone had dropped it there, not as if Boone had been wearing it when he toppled to the ground. On his bristly face was an expression that made Patrick very uneasy.

In the distance, behind Boone, loomed a large desert cactus, the top of which—like Jack's beanstalk—was too high for Patrick to see. It looked as if it were growing out of Boone's shoulder. Patrick narrowed his eyes. He focused on one wicked-looking cactus needle that stuck out against the hard blue of the sky, just above Boone's uppermost arm.

If he was breathing, even shallowly, the shoulder level would rise and the spike would disappear.

It didn't.

Patrick caught his own breath and held it until he nearly burst. He had suddenly realized his fatal mistake.

He had taken a plastic Boone back with him. The living Boone had gone back to England, to Omri's and Patrick's present, in the same instant that Patrick had come here. They must have crossed. That was the meaning of the whooshing sensation of something passing him as he traveled through time and space.

Patrick sat down abruptly, and as abruptly jumped up again. The glassy stones were very hot. Everything was very hot. He felt dizzy. He tottered back a few yards until he was in Boone's shadow, and sank down again to think.

He must have done something to Boone, who'd been clutched tightly in his hand when he climbed into the chest.

Maybe he'd killed him!

No maybe about it. Boone, in the instant of transfer, had fallen down here in the desert. Breathless. Lifeless.

A terrible guilt, backed up by an overwhelming sorrow, threatened Patrick. But, being a very practical boy, he shoved them both roughly to the back of his mind and considered instead his own situation.

He was on his own. No Boone to take care of him.

Minute. Helpless. Miles from anywhere. And at the mercy of the sun and the empty desert.

It seemed a fairly safe bet that soon enough he would follow Boone once again: this time into the oblivion of death.

8.

A Heart Stops Beating

The suspense was awful—the worst of Omri's life.

He watched Matron bending over the still figure in the plaid shirt and chaps. Boone—so real, so very much of a person, and yet so vulnerable that Patrick's hand closing on him in the instant of being swung back through time and space could have squeezed the life out of him.

Omri thought what Patrick would feel, when he came back, if he learned that he had killed Boone. *Killed* him. Crushed him to death. Suddenly Omri knew that it was for Patrick's sake, more than Boone's in a way, that Matron had to breathe life back into that tiny body, as she was now trying to do.

"Matron—"

"Sh!"

She had stopped giving Boone the kiss of life and begun

giving him artificial resuscitation, hands on his ribs, throwing her weight forward and back, panting from the effort she was making.

"Is he—alive?" whispered Omri.

"Yes," she said shortly, between pushes. "Just about."

"What's wrong? Is he—crushed?"

"Crushed? Of course not! He's been—half suffocated—that's all!" She put her ear to his chest again.

"Where's his hat?" said Omri suddenly.

Matron straightened herself with an exclamation.

"His *hat?*" she said sharply. "What in the world does that matter when his heart's stopped?"

"His heart's stopped!" Omri's own heart nearly did the same. "Then he is dead!"

"Not if we can—Wait! You could do it! He needs a good thump on the chest to get it going again! I just haven't the strength. Come here, do exactly as I show you! Now watch!"

Peering at her, he saw her do something with her tiny fingers.

"What—"

She gave an exclamation of exasperation. "Are you blind? It's a flicking movement—flick your finger out from behind your thumb—"

"Oh—like this?"

"Right! Now do it downward—against his chest! No, not so gently—do it hard, thump him, man, thump him!" she cried agitatedly.

Omri flicked his middle finger hard so that his nail struck against Boone's chest, rocking his body.

"Again!"

Omri repeated the movement. Matron then pushed his

finger out of the way and once more laid her ear against Boone's plaid shirtfront.

"Ah!"

"Is it—"

"I do believe—I think—I'm almost certain—YES!" She raised a beaming, sweat-glossed face. "You've done the trick! Well done, oh, well done indeed, you've saved him! Now. Bring me something warm to wrap him in while I go and fix him an injection of heart stimulant. Look—look, he's beginning to breathe normally! What a relief—I was really afraid he was a goner!"

Omri, feeling weak with relief, rushed to hack out another square from his shattered sweater, already jagged-hemmed due to all the miniature blankets he'd cut out of it. Matron hurried up the ramp onto the seed tray and into the longhouse. She emerged at once with a hypodermic syringe and an ampoule so small Omri just had to guess it was there. She knelt beside Boone, now warmly covered, and injected straight into his chest.

"Now listen, young man. We've saved this one between us, but the emergency cases in there are still in desperate need of expert attention. You will really have to secure qualified medical aid."

"Om-RI!"

He turned. Little Bear was standing nearby, arms folded.

"What happen Boone?"

"He's had an accident."

"Ax? Dent? Enemy dent head with tomahawk?"

"No, no. Something else. . . . It's okay, Matron'll take care of him."

"Good." Little Bear bent down and touched Boone's red

hair. Omri felt quite choked up at this tender gesture, until the Indian added, "Sometime I sorry Boone my blood brother."

"Little Bear! Surely you're not still hankering after his scalp?"

The Indian fingered the hair regretfully and grunted. "Fine color, like sugar-tree leaf . . . very bad if other brave get . . ." He gave Boone's head a sharp, possessive pat and straightened up. "Dance finish. You take dead braves, plasstic. Put in ground."

"Little Bear, I can't now. I must go with Emma. Did—did you see her? She—she saw you. I have to make sure she—helps, and doesn't tell."

Little Bear looked troubled.

"Woman tongue stay still like falling water, like grass in wind. . . . You go. Keep hand ready stop mouth of Em-A. First put Little Bear back in longhouse with wife, son."

"You don't want to be sent back to the village yet?"

Little Bear, usually so phlegmatic, suddenly twisted his face, threw up his arms, and turned his body first one way, then another.

"Very bad, need be two place same time! Want be here, not leave hurt braves! Need be there, with tribe! Very bad, one man heart cut in two!"

This was more than Omri could cope with. He lifted the five Indians, including Little Bear, off the table and deposited them hastily on the seed tray. Bright Stars came running out of the longhouse with her baby in her arms, and Little Bear embraced her.

"We'll decide what you should do when I get back," said Omri. He turned to Matron. "Can I leave you?"

"In a good cause—yes."

"Give me an hour."

As he came running downstairs, he sensed at once that Emma had gone.

He felt bereft, though he didn't entirely blame her. Waiting down here by herself, no doubt she had suddenly been overcome with the feeling that it was all too much for her, that she wanted to run off home to her everyday life. But he couldn't let her go. Of course he couldn't. He grabbed his parka and dashed out of the house.

As soon as he turned out of his gate into Hovel Road, Omri smelled trouble.

He saw them halfway down, outside the amusement arcade, a whole crowd of them. He couldn't see Emma, but something in the way the skinheads were crowding around —something in their stance, in the sounds that drifted to him along the street—told him that she was there, in the midst of them, trapped, that they were taunting her—the same mindless bullying treatment he had had from them so often himself. Without his conscious command, his feet drove into a hard run.

He didn't stop to think or give himself time to get scared. He just rammed into them head-on.

A piercing pain blew up like fireworks in his head. He'd completely forgotten his burn! He clutched the place and felt the bandage, and at the same time the circle bent and broke, letting him through, and he saw the faces, first astounded, then twisting into sniggering laughter.

"Cor! If it ain't the old Ayatollah!"

Emma was standing erect and defiant, her lip curled in contempt as she faced the tallest of the gang. Omri recognized him instantly.

"You are just an ugly bullying *creep!*" she threw at him.

"Slag," he sneered. "Nerd—" Then he noticed Omri.

His whole face altered. Unwholesomely pale already, it turned the dead color of putty. His jaw went slack, as if Omri's own fear had erupted and were mirrored in this other face.

"You—" he gasped.

"Yeah, me," said Omri, panting, dry-mouthed. There were so many of them! "You lot leave her alone. Or else."

A concerted jeer rose from the circle.

"Look out, lads! Fall flat on your faces and worship 'im, or 'e's liable to start an 'oly war!"

But their leader—the big youth who'd been going on at Emma—glanced furiously around at his mates, and the jeering laughter died.

He reached up grimy fingers and unconsciously caressed his face, across which, in a diagonal line, were a dozen tiny raw dots.

" 'Ow you done that?" he muttered, his eyes narrowed as he looked at Omri. "I'd give a lot to know 'ow you done what you done to me."

Omri contented himself with a tight little smile. He took Emma by the arm.

"Come on, Em, let's go."

The tall boy gave a kind of twitch of his shaved head. The circle wavered, then gave way and let them through, though not without murmurings of puzzlement and rebellion.

Just as they came clear, Omri had a thought. He paused and reached into his jeans pocket.

He turned casually back. Could they see how his heart was pounding?

"Oh, by the way—" He held out his hand. "I think one of you dropped this."

He held up the penlight that he'd picked up after the burglars' hasty departure.

The tall skinhead reached for it automatically, took hold of it, then suddenly let it go as if it were red-hot. It fell to the pavement, where it rolled into the gutter. Several of the others made a dive for it.

"Leave it!" the leader barked. "Don't touch it! It might blow up in your face!"

Omri stared at him for a moment. That great thieving, bullying lout was really afraid of him. It wasn't entirely a good feeling, but it was better than the other way around, which was the way it had always been before.

Now all the faces looking at him were pallid and nervous. Take away their gang courage, and they really were a pathetic-looking crew. Omri felt the beginnings of a sneer twisting his own mouth, but it felt ugly even from inside so he was glad when Emma tugged his arm.

They walked quickly down to the station, leaving a defeated silence behind them.

9.

Tamsin
Drives A Bargain

By the time Omri and Emma arrived at Emma's house, half of Omri's allotted hour had passed and he was getting panicky.

Emma didn't make things easier.

"What are we going to say about Patrick not coming back?"

Omri liked the way she said "we," making him feel less alone with his problems, but he didn't want to confront this one. How indeed was he to explain Patrick's absence? Perhaps he could play both ends, so to speak, against the middle. If each household—his and Emma's—thought Patrick was in the other one, Patrick might not be missed for some time. But for a really lousy liar like Omri, it was bound to be tricky.

Patrick's mother was practically on the doorstep to meet them.

"Well, where is he?" she asked without even saying hello.

Emma turned to look at Omri expectantly.

"Er—I came to explain," he said. "You see—" He swallowed hard. Her eyes were piercing him. He had to drop his. "We . . . we went into Richmond Park this morning to look for chestnuts. On our bikes."

"Patrick's bike is at home in the country."

"I mean—he used Gillon's. And . . . we were playing—and he got a bit lost, and I got fed up waiting and came home without him. I expect he'll be back soon," he added hastily as Patrick's mother rolled her eyes, gritted her teeth, and uttered a kind of snort.

"How like him to do the disappearing act just when I want him! Doesn't he realize we're going home today? What *am* I supposed to do? I *have* to leave!"

"Couldn't Patrick stay with us for a few days?"

"Don't be so silly. What about school? It's *school* tomorrow!" She was obviously infuriated, and Omri couldn't exactly blame her.

However, there was nothing to be done for the moment. Leaving her seething in the doorway, Emma pulled Omri past and into the small living room.

"Leave Tam to me," she whispered. "She absolutely hates you for some reason."

Omri felt rather hurt, even though it was entirely mutual.

Tamsin was slumped in front of a small television set, watching some middle-of-the-day rubbish. Her leg, encased from foot to knee in a white plaster cast, was resting on a pouffe. She didn't even look up as they came in. Emma coughed.

"Hey, Tam, want to add to your skiing fund?"

"Fat chance of skiing when I'm like this," she said sourly.

"You could go at Easter. Best snow's always in April."

Tamsin looked up sharply at that. Seeing Omri, her eyes narrowed.

"You look a right idiot in that bandage," she remarked. "Did someone give you a clout?"

"Not since you," Omri retorted.

Tamsin had the grace to blush. She turned back to her sister.

"What about my skiing fund?"

"Well, you know your birthday models—"

"I already said no," said Tamsin. "I won't swap."

Emma shrugged with wondrous carelessness. "I just fancy one or two of them, that's all. I'd buy them off you."

Tamsin glanced at Omri again. "Is this anything to do with *him*?"

"Who? Oh! No, of course not. You know I wanted them yesterday."

Tamsin's eyes looked beady. "If you wait till tomorrow, you can buy the same set at the model shop."

"I need them now," Emma had to say, though she tried to sound careless.

Tamsin uncurled herself slowly and frowningly. Without a word she heaved her cast onto the floor and stumped out of the room. Omri almost felt sorry for her, but this charitable impulse was soon to pass. Emma nudged him. They waited.

After a few minutes Tamsin returned, carrying the box Omri recognized from last night.

She opened it and displayed the contents. The figures, held to a cardboard backing with elastic, dangled tantalizingly before their eyes. Omri's flew to the surgeon in green operating-theater gear, complete with table and tiny instruments, mere pinhead blobs. There were two other doctors, one in a white coat with a stethoscope, the other, also in green, who was evidently part of the surgical team. It was as much as Omri could do to restrain his hand from darting toward them.

Instead he thrust both hands into his pockets and turned away to gaze blindly at the TV set while negotiations between the twins proceeded.

They seemed to take forever. Somehow Tamsin could sense that Emma's casualness masked some urgent desire for the medical models. In the end, though, when the price had reached astronomical heights, several times what they'd have cost in the shops, and Omri was beginning to despair of Tamsin's greed ever being satisfied, the bargain was struck.

The little figures were detached, the better part of Omri's fiver handed over, and Emma and Omri found themselves out in the hall again, tiptoeing toward the front door.

"Where do you think you're going, Emma?"

They stopped cold. Emma shut her eyes. It was *her* mother this time, the sister of Patrick's mother and just such another, it seemed.

Omri thought, *Good, she'll have to stop here, and that means I won't have to be bothered about her.* She'd served her purpose, and surely the fewer people who were involved, the better. But he glanced sideways at Emma's face, and to his own astonishment he heard himself saying, "Can Emma come back to my place for lunch?"

Emma's mother said, "How will she get home?"
"My dad'll run her back,"'said Omri glibly.
"Before dark."
"Of course."
"Oh—all right then. I suppose . . ."
They gave her no time to think twice. They were out and
down the street as fast as they could run.

"Now," said Emma as they sat on the train going back to
Omri's district, "I want to know everything."
Omri groaned inwardly. He'd managed to fend off her
questions on the way to her house, but there was something
in her voice that told him that no amount of fending would
work now.
He turned in his seat to face her.
"Listen, Em. You've got to swear yourself to secrecy."
"Okay," she agreed readily.
"No, not like that. It's not just a game. You don't know how
hard it's going to be to keep this to yourself."
"With Tam for a sister, I've learned how to keep secrets,
don't worry."
Omri slumped back against the train seat. He'd have to
trust her—it was too late not to.
"Okay, then. You saw them. They're real, they're no
dream and no game. There's proper magic in this world, to
do with time, and—and souls of people that can travel in
time and from place to place, and enter things like toys, and
make them come to life. And we can travel too. I mean our
—our spirits can. That's where Patrick is. He's time-travel-
ing."

Emma was staring at him.

"Why's it a secret?"

"Can't you see? If grown-ups knew . . ."

"Oh. Yes. Not just grown-ups. If *Tam* knew . . . !"

"We wouldn't be allowed to keep it. It works—I might as well tell you this—with a special key. And a little bathroom cupboard, and my oak chest. All that would all be taken away. There'd be newspapers, TV—"

Emma sat up straight, her eyes alight.

"Would we be on TV?"

Omri's heart plummeted.

"Em, you mustn't. You must not think like that. Yes, we'd be on TV, and everything would be *ruined.*"

Emma sat back, frowning. He could see her thinking. He had the feeling she wasn't particularly used to thinking seriously, any more than he'd been himself, before all this started.

They hurried along the length of Hovel Road unmolested. The skinhead gang had gone, home for lunch presumably. As they half-ran, Emma said, "Where exactly has Patrick gone?"

"Well," said Omri, "I'm pretty worried about that." And he explained how the key worked, as best he could. "You have to take someone or something real, or alive, with you, if you want to go to a specific place and time. Like, when I went back to the Indian village last night, I took a pair of Bright Stars' moccasins in my pocket. Patrick took Boone, but he forgot the rules, and as he *went,* Boone *came back.*"

"So he could be anywhere, just—floating about in time?"

"I don't know. The only thing is—"

"What?"

"Well, it's only a slight hope, but I'm sure Boone—I mean his plastic figure—was wearing his hat when Patrick set off. Maybe the hat got caught up in some—some sort of time current and attached itself to Patrick, in which case he went to Texas after all, because that's where the hat belongs."

"Complicated, in' it?" said Emma, doing a London accent.

Omri wasn't into accents, so he just said feelingly, "You said it." But he glanced at her appreciatively. She was taking it pretty reasonably. And she was fun. And it wasn't bad at all, having someone to help now Patrick had PO'd.

As they reached the house, it occurred to Omri as ironic that the whole business with Patrick's going back in time had come up in the first place so Patrick wouldn't have to go home—so he could stay and *help Omri.*

Huh, thought Omri. *Fine friend.*

But Patrick *was* his friend. And even at times when Omri was fed up with him, like now, he still liked him enough to care what was happening to him.

Omri and Emma hurried up to Omri's room. Omri's first act was to bend over the longhouse and call softly.

"Matron!"

She came out. She didn't bustle quite so briskly now. Her starched apron was soiled, and her magnificent cap was limp and askew. She looked very tired.

"Well? What luck?"

"How's Boone?" asked Omri. "How are the others?"

"Your cowboy friend is a bit better, though he's still unconscious. He's breathing normally, but he's badly bruised. The Indians . . ." Her shoulders slumped a little. "One is hanging between life and death. Bullet in the trachea, another in the leg. I need help desperately."

"We've brought you some." She straightened up with relief; even the erstwhile magnificent cap seemed to stiffen a little.

"Well, what are we waiting for! Let's get to it!"

Emma meanwhile had lost no time in consigning the medical team to the cupboard. But just before Omri closed the door, Emma, peering at the seed tray, suddenly said, "Whose are these sweet little horses?"

Sweet little horses! *God!* thought Omri, gritting his teeth. But he kept his temper and said, "The brown one's Little Bear's. The black one belongs to the cowboy."

"Can I put the cowboy's one back in the cupboard?"

"What *for?*"

"Well, I want to see how it works in reverse. And you said Patrick might be in Boone's time. Maybe he needs a horse."

"Don't be stupid, Patrick will be small, like the little people are here! What use would a socking great horse be to him? He couldn't possibly ride it."

"Still, let me."

Omri couldn't be bothered making any more objections. Emma tenderly lifted the little black horse between finger and thumb and put it in the cupboard.

"Will it go *back* at the same time as the doctors come *forward?*"

"Yes! Oh, do let's get on with it!" said Omri impatiently.

The door was closed on the live horse and the plastic men. The key was turned. Emma, her ear to the mirrored door, grinned ecstatically at Omri: She could hear tiny voices questioning each other in the darkness. Her hand went to the key, but Omri stopped her.

"Listen," he said quietly. "One of the tricky things is,

when they see us, trying to get them to believe it and not think they've lost their minds. Our best bet with these modern people is to get Matron to explain."

Matron was ready and eager, impatient to get the team out and to work on her patients.

"Leave it to me," she said. "Just let me in that cupboard."

"But what will you say?"

"I've thought it all out," she said. "Most men, if you just tell them what to do in a businesslike fashion, will follow directions without thinking about it. One proceeds on the assumption that they'll do as they're told, and they do. However, they may be forced to think a bit if they see you two, so I suggest you keep out of the way." She nipped back into the longhouse, presumably to make sure everything was in perfect order, then hurried out, down the ramp and across to the cupboard.

"Right you are," she said. "Open sesame!"

As she slid through the partly open door, Omri put his hand stealthily in at the top and lifted out the plastic figure of Boone's horse.

"Here," he muttered to Emma. "This was your daft idea—you'd better take care of it."

She took the little figure from him and looked into its plastic face.

"He's happy to be home," she said mysteriously. "Now Patrick isn't completely on his own, anyway."

10.

A Rough Ride

Patrick brooded, his chin on his hands, his elbows on his bent knees. He was sitting in the massive shadow of Boone's corpse (not that Patrick allowed himself to think this in so many words, but he was quite sure in the back of his mind that that's what it was), trying to think, and at the same time trying not to think. The two conflicting efforts canceled each other out. His mind was a blank. His eyes were unfocused.

Suddenly they did focus. They focused on something he hadn't noticed before. Heaven knows why, because it was absolutely enormous. A vast black mountain range on the horizon. *And it was moving.*

It was heaving. It was threshing. One part of it, at the far left-hand end of the range, was rearing itself up. Up, up—into the sky!

Patrick sprang to his feet and shaded his eyes. The vast black mass was erupting in a series of bounding curves and angular jolts. It was awesome, like witnessing the primeval forces that created the world, throwing up volcanic ranges from the hot laval center of the earth.

But abruptly Patrick lost his sense of awe and terror. He threw back his head and laughed.

Because now the mountain range finished heaving and stood upright on four titanic legs, revealed for what it was.

It was a horse!

It must have been lying motionless in what to Patrick was the distance—its spirit, or whatever, somewhere far away in place and time. And now it had come back to itself, and stood up and—"Cripes!"—it was lumbering toward him!

Patrick ran. He ran back toward the sheltering bulk of Boone. He hid himself under a vast flap that was the lapel of Boone's plaid shirt collar, tucked under his bristly chin.

As Patrick ducked behind this flannel "curtain," he heard a strange, almost musical sound, like a wheezing groan. A huge fleshy knob just above the neck band moved—along— then back, making the shirt collar shiver and shift. At first Patrick had no notion what was happening, but as the groaning sounds went on and the motion of the lump in Boone's throat continued, he suddenly realized.

Frightened though he was—the thundering tread of those colossal hooves was shaking the ground like a series of earthquakes as they approached—Patrick registered with an incredulous sense of relief that the bristly skin above the shirt was warm, and that the groaning sounds were rasping breaths, and that the lump was Boone's Adam's apple.

"Boone, you're alive!" Patrick breathed, feeling a sudden

intense happiness. He almost kissed the Adam's apple as it slid past him. But then he sensed the horse's tremendous head coming down on him, and he crouched, trembling, behind the collar.

He felt a rush of hot, powerfully horse-scented breath that came right through the thick flannel. Then there was a loud sound like the rumble of distant thunder as the horse blew through its lips. The horse was smelling Boone. Next it nudged the cowboy's shoulder with its nose, causing another sort of earthquake that had Patrick rolling over on the stones.

He peered out from behind the flap.

The first thing he saw, vast as it was, was recognizable as a hoof. The sloping horny part was about twice Patrick's height, with a fringe of coarse black hairs hanging over the top of it.

Patrick never knew afterward what possessed him to take the action he now took almost unthinkingly. He knew he had to get out of this desert unless he wanted to die of heatstroke, thirst, or the attentions of wild creatures. He needed to escape. So, instinctively, he acted.

He took a run at the hoof, scrambled halfway up the hard slope on hands and feet, grabbed a handful of the coarse black hair, and hauled himself up to a kind of ledge where the gigantic leg bone started.

There he almost panicked. The hoof he was on was planted firmly in the sand, but at some stage it would start to move, probably very fast. Patrick looked at the tempting slope to the ground and nearly slid straight back down again to short-term safety.

But then he thought, *No. I must get out of here and this is the only way.*

He hurriedly took several of the long black hairs of the horse's fetlock, twisted them together, and knotted them firmly around his waist. Then he reached as high as he could and took a strong grip with both hands on more of the hairs, at the same time bracing his sneakers on the ridge at the top of the hoof.

He felt surprisingly secure, ready for anything. So he thought. He had absolutely no idea of the terrifying experience that was in store for him when the horse, getting no response from its prostrate master, abruptly threw up its head, turned swiftly, and started to gallop across the desert sand.

Patrick had always loved terrifying rides at fairs, the scarier the better—the centrifugal drum was one of his favorites, and that rocket that spins and plunges and twists and whirls around all at the same time. But no fair ride ever dreamed up by an ingenious showman could compare with standing braced on the hoof of a giant horse as it races over hot sand.

Over and over again the great hoof would rise in the air, leaving Patrick's stomach far below, and sweep through a monstrous arc that had Patrick dangling high above the sand. If he hadn't tied himself on securely, nothing could have saved him. The hoof would bend and turn in such a way that his body would be twisted and flung almost upside down, before the hoof plunged down again to strike the ground with a sickening jar. The speed alone was enough to make most people faint, but Patrick grimly hung on.

Yet his handgrips became weaker and weaker as the

crazy, fantastic, nerve-and-bone-racking ride went on and on. To make matters worse, dust and stones, struck up from the ground by the flying hooves, flew through the air and pelted Patrick all over. He didn't feel these at the time. Every bit of his mind, and every muscle and sinew, were preoccupied with the single task of holding on. He didn't know that his eyes were screwed shut, that his breath was coming in jolts, that with every breath he uttered a cry or a groan. For him, all was sickening motion, whirling blackness, jarring blows, and absolute terror.

By the time it stopped, he was almost unconscious. His handholds had given way, though one wrist was still held by a tangle of hairs. He hung from this, and the tie at his waist, like a rag doll. His whole body was covered with bruises; his throat was choked with dust so that he could scarcely draw breath.

Gradually he came back to his senses and straightened up painfully. He opened his eyes with difficulty—they were caked with wind tears and dust. He peered dazedly around him.

There seemed to be a lot going on. Noise, movement. At his level, near the ground, he could see a lot of other huge hooves, moving and stamping. The ground itself was not sand, but packed earth. There was a very strong horse smell, probably dung. He raised his eyes and saw some vast posts and rails, and the heads of a number of horses besides his own. Straight before him was a wooden cliff about six times Patrick's height.

The hoof he was still attached to lifted and made a pawing movement that brought it level with the top of this cliff. Patrick then saw what it was—the edge of a wooden sidewalk. Now he could see gigantic feet, some in cowboy boots with villainous spurs attached, others in lighter footwear all but covered by long skirts, striding past with vast steps that thundered on the boards.

Patrick took advantage of the horse's hoof being, for the moment, planted on the sidewalk, to free himself—just as well. No sooner had he slid down the sloping hoof to the wooden floor than his horse's head swept down and its giant slabs of teeth, as big as tombstones, bit scratchingly into its fetlock, exactly where Patrick had been tied a moment before!

It was dangerous to try to cross the sidewalk—any one of those mighty thundering feet could crush him on the way. From his viewpoint it was like trying to make it across a ten-lane highway during rush hour.

But he couldn't stay here. Already the horse was snuffling at him, nearly sucking him up into its cavernous nostril. Patrick ran out of range and found himself surrounded by the feet. He must get out of here! He must find someone to help him!

Just then he saw some boots coming to a standstill right beside him. Curiously, they were not brown or black, but bright red and shiny. One scarlet lace had come untied and hung down to the ground.

Patrick put his head back as far as it would go and looked upward.

He could see a whole sky of frothy white petticoats and the hem of a red satin dress, a long way above him. It was a lady.

She had come up onto the sidewalk from the dirt road and

had paused for a moment. Again he acted without thinking, grabbing the red bootlace and heaving himself up—though he ached in every limb—onto the arched instep where he could find comfortable and safe refuge among the crossed red laces and metal-ringed lace holes.

I'm safe! he thought.

That was his opinion.

11.

Ruby Lou

The feet moved on, across the sidewalk, not along it. This ride was quite pleasantly unexciting after the other. Patrick heard a thud as the lady boldly pushed open some swinging doors. Then she walked inside.

The street sounds—the clopping of hooves, the thudding of feet, the sound of wagons and voices and barking dogs—changed to other sounds, familiar to Patrick from Western films. He knew at once he was in a saloon. There was a piano playing a jangly tune, and lots of voices shouting and singing cheerfully. The smell in the air was of alcohol, cigarette smoke, cheap scent, sweat, sawdust, and leather.

The lady who was unwittingly carrying Patrick made straight for the bar. She rested on a rail the foot he was on. It was dark down there, and the smell was pretty bad. Patrick wondered how he could attract the lady's attention, or whether it would be fatal to do so. He could hear her voice among the other voices.

"An' who's gonna buy me a drink, boys? Ruby Lou don't take kindly to drinkin' alone, and she never, never pays for her own liquor!"

There was no shortage of offers. Patrick saw men's feet crowding around the red shiny boots and heard the jovial cries of male voices above, yelling, "Yea, Lou! I'll buy ya a dozen!" "Good ol' Ruby Lou! Have one on me, sweetheart!"

"Okay, okay, don't crowd me now!" Ruby Lou said sharply, and the boots shuffled reluctantly a step backwards.

Patrick could hear the noisy *glug-glug-glug* of whisky being poured from a bottle, and he could smell it, too. Whisky made him think at once of Boone, and so it seemed a quite incredible coincidence when Ruby Lou's voice suddenly echoed his thoughts.

"Hey, where's my favorite fella?" she cried. "Where's Boone? Boone always makes me laugh!"

"Boo-Hoo Boone? Make ya cry, more like!" jeered one man, and the rest all burst into mock boo-hooing.

Ruby Lou took offense on Boone's behalf.

"Ain't nothin' wrong with a soft heart," she said. "Trouble with you boys is, you ain't got hearts, or if ya have, they ain't got no more feelin's in 'em than chunks o' rock! It don't mean he ain't got guts, neither! Gimme a man with feelin's, even if he do git through two-three of my best lace-edged hankies every time we hear a hard-luck story!"

She shouldn't have said that. The notion of Boone mopping up his tears with lace hankies was too much, even for Patrick. As the crowd of men above him burst their sides laughing, Patrick, below on the red leather, laughed too until, weakened as he was, he slipped.

He felt himself sliding down the side of the boot, and grabbed the red bootlace. This broke his fall, but it gave Ruby Lou's foot a tug.

As he climbed back up to his perch, he saw her huge hand coming down toward him. He crouched low in the opening of her boot. He didn't realize that he was digging his hands and feet into her instep until he heard her say peevishly, "I got me a itch on my tootsy. This saloon is turnin' into a real flea circus!"

And her fingers, with their sharp nails, began to prod around the lacings. Patrick tried to dodge, but suddenly one finger fell on him, squeezing him hard against a metal-rimmed lace hole so that he thought his back would break and he writhed frantically to free himself.

"Hey! This is some flea that's bitin' me!" she squealed. She picked Patrick up between finger and thumb, and the next second he was being swung through the air.

Ruby Lou set Patrick down on the bar.

All at once the noise in his immediate vicinity stopped. The sudden startled silence spread backwards until even the piano player faltered and faded out. Patrick stood ankle-deep in a puddle of whisky (the fumes nearly knocked him out), looking upward fearfully at the semicircle of enormous faces around him, waiting helplessly for one or another of them to raise a meaty hand and swat him flat.

No one did.

Instead the bartender, who was standing on the other side of the bar with a bottle of whisky in his hand, dropped it. It fell on the bar with a (to Patrick) ear-numbing clunk, making the whole bar jump, and to his horror began rolling slowly toward him, spilling whisky as it went.

Seeing it approach, Patrick raced to get out of its way. He ran as fast as his aching legs would let him, hearing the huge bottle trundling along the wooden bar behind him, nearer and nearer. Surely, surely it must soon roll over him like a steamroller!

But luckily for him it didn't roll straight. Abruptly he heard the noise stop as it reached the edge. There was a brief pause before it shattered on the barroom floor.

He stopped running and turned, panting.

The eyes of every person in the saloon were fixed on him, and every bloodshot eye was popping. Vast mouths hung loosely open; bristly faces were paper-white or mottled purple.

"Wh-wh-what IS that?" gibbered one man at last, pointing at him with a trembling finger. "Boys, am I seein' things, or —is—that—a li'l—tiny—ackshul—fella?"

Before anyone could reply, Patrick sensed a quick movement behind him. He spun around instinctively, to find himself staring straight up the barrel of a six-shooter.

"Whatever it is, I don't like it!" growled the owner, and fired.

The noise alone nearly killed Patrick, though the gun wavered at the last second (did a red shiny bulk lurch against the shooting arm?). The bullet ploughed into the top of the bar right next to him, splintering the wood.

The next moment, complete chaos broke out.

The barman, who had reeled back against the enormous mirror which reflected the whole room, suddenly and silently sank out of sight behind the bar. This seemed to act as

a signal. The giants at the bar just went crazy, bumping into each other, throwing punches, firing their guns at random in a series of horrific explosions. One of the light fixtures was hit and came crashing down, causing total panic.

There was a concerted mass movement backwards, away from the bar, followed by a rising thunder of boots stampeding on boards, causing massive vibrations that had Patrick involuntarily dancing up and down on the bar. Twenty or thirty men cut a parting through the smoky air as they forced their way out through the narrow doorway.

One little fellow, the piano player, tripped, fell, and was ruthlessly trampled underfoot by the rest. When they'd all gone, he lay there for a moment, winded, before picking himself up. He gave one terrified backward look toward the bar, cast his eyes upward as if in prayer, let out a weird sound, and fled, clutching his hat.

The swinging doors went *whump-whump-whump*, backwards and forwards, on emptiness, before coming to a stop.

Patrick gingerly took his fingers out of his ears and glanced around the saloon, expecting to find himself alone. But he wasn't, not quite.

Standing a few yards down the bar, the exact distance that Patrick had run away from the bottle, was a giantess with blond hair and a rather low-cut red satin dress. It was hard for Patrick to judge, but she looked quite pretty. She wore a sparkling necklace of red stones and dangly earrings and a very funny expression as she looked at him.

She reached out suddenly and picked up her small glass, which she emptied down her throat in one gulp. Then she plonked it back on the bar and said, "Well, li'l fella, you sure would make a good temperance preacher! I ain't never seen a saloon empty so fast! Thanks for lettin' 'em buy me a drink first. I needed it!"

She laughed a little crazily and drank someone else's drink that had been abandoned. Then she beckoned to him.

"Come here, li'l Jack the Giant Killer, come to Ruby Lou! C'mon, I won't hurt ya, I just wanna make sure you ain't somethin' I dreamed."

Patrick walked back along the vast shiny expanse of the bar toward her. His legs were shaking, and his feet squelched in his whisky-sodden sneakers. He had no idea whether he would be safe with her or not, but he couldn't manage alone, and who else was there? Anyway, she liked Boone, so she couldn't be all bad.

Ruby Lou's face, brightly painted, came down until it was level with his. He could smell her perfume. Well, it was better than the whisky, anyhow.

"Okay, kid, let's have it. What gives? I ain't drunk, and I ain't that crazy, and you look to me like the smallest human critter that ever was in the length and breadth o' Texas!"

"Actually I'm English," said Patrick, feeling silly but not knowing what else to say.

"English! Is that s'posed to be a introduction, or a explanation? I heard it was kind of a small island, but I never knew the men from there was only three inches tall!"

Patrick blushed. "I'm not exactly a typical English person," he said. "You see—"

"Speak up, kid, that's a teeny tiny voice box you got there, and I'll admit it to ya, I'm a mite deef from all the shoutin' an' shootin' that goes on around here!"

Patrick cleared his throat. "Sorry!" he bellowed. Then he shouted, "Listen, I need help."

"You coulda fooled me, buster!"

"Not just for myself. For Boone."

"Say!" Her face lit up. "You a friend o' Billy Boone's?"

"Yes. We're old friends. And he's in trouble."

"Yeah? Tell me somethin' new. When ain't he!"

"He's lying out in the desert unconscious. I think someone should go out there and get him."

"Can you show me where he is?"

"No. But maybe his horse can—it's outside, or it was."

Ruby Lou straightened up and looked around. The saloon was still empty, but peeping over the top of the swinging doors was a pair of eyes under a well-pulled-down hat.

"Hey, Reverend! Come in here, it's okay!"

The doors slowly parted, and the little piano player who had been trampled on sidled hesitantly in.

"I want ya to meet m' new sidekick—er—"

"Pat," said Patrick, thinking that "Patrick" sounded a bit of a feeble name for the Wild West.

"Pat—this is Tickle. His real name's the Reverend Godfrey Tickson, and he has a past you wouldn't believe to look at him now, but we call him Tickle 'cause he tickles the ivories. *Plays the piano,* get it? Plays real good, too, especially hymns! Only not now, eh, Tick? I got somethin' important fer ya to do. Is your buggy handy?"

"Yeah, Ruby," said the Reverend Tickle in a squeaky voice. "It's right outside."

"Me 'n' Pat, here, is goin' fer a little ride on Boone's hoss, and you're gonna drive right along behind us. What say?" She patted his chubby cheek.

"Sure, Ruby," squeaked Tickle, nearly nodding his hat off. "If you say so!"

Ruby Lou's white hand with its glittering rings swept Patrick up. Gasping, he felt for the first time how the "little people" had felt when he and Omri had handled them. He hoped he'd always picked up Boone as gently as Ruby Lou did him, but he doubted it, remembering some times when he'd stuffed him in his jeans pocket and not been at all bothered if the cowboy was frightened or uncomfortable.

"Where'd ya favor ridin', pal? Not on my shoe again, huh? My shoulder? Naw, bit slippery. . . . Hey, I know a nice safe place!"

And before Patrick knew what was happening, she had thrust him into the front of her dress. Which, once he got over his slight embarrassment, was just like being in the front row of the dress circle in a theater. Or maybe in the bow of a very large ship.

Ruby Lou slapped Tickle's hand away when he reached for one of the abandoned drinks, and swept out of the saloon with Patrick just ahead of her like a miniature figurehead on an old-fashioned galleon. She got him to point out Boone's horse, and before you could say "Howdy" she had stuck her high-heeled boot in the heavy stirrup and in a flurry of petticoats and red satin had swung herself into the saddle.

Patrick found himself at skyscraper height, with a fantastic view of a street that was somehow familiar. Then he remembered. Of course! It was the street Boone had drawn for them that time in the art lesson at school! There was the jail, and across the way the livery stables, the dirt road with the horses and wagons, and the doctor's sign, and the general store. The only thing there wasn't was people, though he thought he saw a few curtains twitch in some windows, and the door of the sheriff's office hastily closing.

Tickle meanwhile had hurried to where his horse and buggy were parked and climbed onto the driver's seat, picking up the reins and giving them a shake.

"Praise the Lord, I'm ready t' go, Ruby!" he called in his squeaky voice.

"Okay, fellas!" She kicked the horse, who reared a little, giving Patrick a fright, but Ruby sat her mount as steady as a rock.

"Git on there, hoss! Find Boone!" cried the intrepid Ruby Lou. And the next moment they were galloping down the empty street, leaving Tickle to follow in a cloud of dust.

12.

Caught
Red-Handed

Boone came to that afternoon.

Matron had been exceedingly busy since the surgical team came. She hustled and bustled them across to the seed tray, chatting to them all the time in an isn't-this-interesting-and-also-perfectly-normal sort of voice, and before they knew it they were doing their stuff in a makeshift operating theater with the aid of a powerful torch and relays of tiny containers.

It was Emma's job to keep these coming, though she gave them to Bright Stars to carry in to the team. One lot contained boiling water with a few drops of disinfectant in it. The other lot contained boiling water with tea, sugar, and milk in it. (On one occasion Matron apparently mistook the one for the other, and a great deal of coughing and spluttering ensued.)

As Boone didn't need an operation, he had been estab-

lished in a bed, which Emma, under Omri's guidance, made
of a large Swan Vestas matchbox filled with neatly folded
Kleenex and a small pincushion pillow, set up in a far corner
of the seed tray out of sight of the longhouse and its occupants. He was watched over by Bright Stars, and occasionally visited by Little Bear, who would stray near the bed as if
by accident and peer at Boone's face scowlingly before
stamping off again with a grunt of disfavor.

But at last Bright Stars called to Omri and Emma, who
were just returning from the garden after conducting a brief
burial service over the paper packet of plastic figures.
(Omri's family were not churchgoers, but Emma managed a

prayer of sorts and even thought of putting some tiny flowers on the grave.)

"Boone wake!" Bright Stars said, shifting her baby's slight
weight from one arm to the other. Her face was wreathed in
smiles. She was very fond of Boone, since he had stood by to
help her during the birth of her baby.

Omri and Emma leaned close to the matchbox bed and
saw that, sure enough, Boone had opened his eyes and was
trying to sit up. When he saw Omri looming over him, his
ginger-bristly face broke into a soppy grin.

"Hi there, pardner," he said rather croakily. "Whut happened t' me this time? Did that there sneaky redskin var-
mint shoot another arrow into me, or whut?"

"I'm afraid it was Patrick," confessed Omri. "He didn't
mean it—he just squeezed you too tight."

"Yeah? That'd explain why m' ribs feels like they're
broke."

"Well, they're not, just bruised, but you nearly suffocated."

Boone paled.

"Suffocated! Ya mean, like when they string you up? Geez,
that's allus bin m' worst nightmare, kickin' the bucket that-
a-way! Never woulda thought of ol' Pat bein' so dawgoned
careless! Whur is the kid, anyhow? An' who's this?" he
added, suddenly noticing Emma.

"This is Emma, Boone. She's a friend of ours. Emma, this is
Boone. He's a cowboy from Texas."

Emma stretched out her hand, and Boone solemnly took
hold of the nail of one finger and shook it.

"A real privilege, ma'am," he said courteously. He stared
at her for a moment. "Y' know, with that fair hair o' yorn,

and them eyes blue as the midday sky, ya sure remind me of a lady o' mah acquaintance. . . . A' course, you're a mite younger 'n she is. . . ." He stared a while longer, and then shook himself and said brightly, "Hey, Ah'm feelin' better every minute. Y' know, thur ain't nothing like bein' close to a beautiful female fer bringing a red-blooded dyin' man back t' th' land o' the livin'! Unless it's . . ." And he gave a meaningful swallow.

Omri sighed and glanced at Emma.

"You want a drink," he said resignedly.

"Jest a li'l shot," Boone wheedled, indicating the minutest possible portion between finger and thumb. "Best cure there is fer suffocation."

"Oh, okay," said Omri, laughing. "I'll fetch you some. Emma, you chat with him, tell him where Patrick is—that ought to keep his mind off his thirst."

Omri went downstairs to the living room where the drinks cupboard was. His father was no drinker, but he always kept a bottle of scotch and some wine and beer handy, together with glasses of the appropriate sizes and shapes. Omri chose a tiny liqueur glass and was just pouring a small portion of scotch into it when his father walked into the room and caught him red-handed.

"Omri? What on earth are you up to?"

The question was not angry, merely incredulous. Omri stood there with the whisky bottle in one hand and the tiny glass in the other, the very picture of guilt.

"I—I—I—I'm pouring a drink."

"That's the wrong glass for scotch," said his father, as if he couldn't think of anything else to say. He walked across, took the bottle out of Omri's hand, and replaced the top. There was a silence, and then he said, "Well, you've poured it, you might as well drink it."

Omri stared at the brown liquid in the glass. He wanted to say, "It's not for me," or, "I don't want it," but he knew that if he did, more questions, unanswerable questions, would be sure to follow. So he took a deep breath, and, with a feeling like despair, he swallowed it in one gulp.

The stuff was *horrible*. It seemed to stick in his throat, making him choke. His eyes sprouted tears. When it finally went down, it burned all the way and hit his unsuspecting stomach like a small depth charge.

He was aware that his father was watching him curiously.

"You're evidently not really into hard liquor," he remarked, looking at Omri's scarlet face and teary eyes.

Omri said nothing.

"Just an experiment, was it?" his father persisted in a man-to-man tone.

"Sort of," croaked Omri.

"Well, try anything once, that's my motto too. *Just* once, in this case, okay?" And he put the bottle away firmly.

Omri moved toward the door, trying to get rid of the filthy taste in his mouth. Just as he got there, his father said, "I think it's time I drove them back."

"Who? Oh! Emma, you mean."

"And Patrick."

"Patrick?" repeated Omri, startled.

"He is up in your room, isn't he?"

"Er—yes. But he's—asleep."

"What do you mean?"

"He was dead tired and he fell asleep and—well, I thought he might stay the night," gabbled Omri.

"Is that okay with his mother?"

Omri mumbled something and then said, "I'll tell Emma to come down."

Later Emma made a secret phone call to Omri from her home, to say that she'd told Patrick's mother that Patrick had returned safely to Omri's after his "bicycle ride," so tired he'd fallen asleep right away. And that, though annoyed, Patrick's mother had resigned herself to staying in town for another night.

"I'll just give him tonight," said Omri. "What he said about staying a week is ridiculous. I'll bring him back in the morning."

Emma said nothing for a moment, and then said, "I *hated* having to leave. I don't want to miss anything. Will you please give my love to Boone and Bright Stars and Little Bear. And the baby. And Matron."

"Matron wouldn't appreciate it," said Omri. "She's above all that." But something in the intensity of feeling in Emma's voice pleased him. "I'll see you at school tomorrow," he went on. "And don't forget. Not a word to anyone. No exceptions. Promise."

And Emma replied, "I already did promise," but just the same, Omri hardly slept all night.

13.

Mr. Johnson
Smells A Rat

Next day was Monday. School.

Omri got up very early after a restless night. Little Bear didn't have to wake him, for once.

The first thing he did was open the chest. Patrick was exactly as before—chill-fleshed, but breathing shallowly. Omri crouched on his heels, staring in at him. He knew what he should do. What he must do, really. Anyway he was dying to hear what had been happening in Texas—if indeed that was where Patrick had wound up. It was just that Omri didn't want to interrupt a great adventure, if there was one going on.

Nevertheless, he closed the lid and put his hand on the key with its red satin ribbon.

"Young man! I need some assistance."

It was Matron in her most commanding mood.

"Could it wait, Matron?"

"No. Some of these men are so much better they can go back where they belong. They're just taking up beds, not to mention my time. Come along, I've marshaled them outside that cupboard of yours—now get them on their way."

Omri stood up. The Indians, about nine of them, many with bandaged limbs or heads, one on crutches made of matchsticks, stood near the door of the cupboard. Little Bear and Bright Stars were with them.

"Is it okay if they go back, Little Bear?"

"Good go back. In village much need do. Each brave have work, enough for many."

"Do you want to go with them?" asked Omri with a heavy heart.

Little Bear looked up at him.

"I think much of go back or stay. I wish this and this. So I choose. You send Little Bear back now. Then when sun go, you bring here again. I see village. Then come back see hurt braves."

"Great idea, you can almost be in two places at once! Will you take Bright Stars with you?"

"Yes take wife. Take son. Omri bring Little Bear back when sun go."

Omri felt a bit confused about the logistics of all this, but he nodded, and he and Little Bear touched hands.

He opened the cupboard. With some help from Matron and each other, the Indians scrambled over the bottom rim. Little Bear helped Bright Stars in. She cast a tender look back at Omri and waved to him.

Omri then "borrowed" the key from the chest and dispatched them. Why did he feel sad about this parting that was to be only for one day? He took the plastic figures from the cupboard and put them safely in his pocket.

Matron gave a sigh of satisfaction.

"We're not going to lose any more now," she said. "The others are all on the mend."

"What did the team think of it all?"

Matron permitted herself a smirk.

"Well, as the Bard says, 'Conscience does make cowards of us all'! I think each of them thought he'd probably had too much to drink, and none of them liked to admit it to the others, so they just got on with the job as per my orders. I mean suggestions."

"I suppose you were up all night, after we sent them back?"

"Let's say I didn't get a lot of sleep. Never mind. All in a night's work."

"You're wonderful," said Omri sincerely.

"Pish, tush, and likewise pooh," said Matron, dismissing the compliment, but he had seen a blush of pleasure spread over those craggy features. "What about a cuppa? Can't start the day without my tea."

"An' Ah cain't start mine without mah cawfee!" chimed in Boone's voice. Omri had fixed him up with a little "house" made of Lego and put it out of sight behind the cupboard, so Boone could get a good night's sleep, away from the seed tray with all the hospital-like hustle and bustle.

Now Omri lifted the roof off. Boone was sitting bolt upright in bed, looking ready for anything. "Ah'm more 'n a mite hungry, too, so as Ah been de-prived of m' likker, don't you go forgettin' some powerful vittles!" Omri had had trou-

ble with him the night before when he'd returned without
any whisky.

He hurried down to the kitchen and fetched as many
"powerful vittles" as he could readily lay hands on, while
boiling the kettle for tea and coffee. He wished Emma were
here. He felt beleaguered, having to do everything himself.
He wasn't sure he'd got his priorities right, seeing that everyone was fed before he did anything about Patrick. As he
tiptoed back upstairs, he thought he'd see to that as soon as
he was dressed.

But hardly was he back in his room than he was alarmed to
hear footsteps rattling up the attic stairs.

"Hey, Omri! Wake up, you're on the news!"

It was Gillon, banging on his door. Omri hastily heaped
some junk onto the top of the chest and opened the bedroom door a crack.

"What are you going on about?"

"It was on my clock radio. Radio London. They just an-
nounced the winners of the story competition!"

Omri was speechless. He'd forgotten about winning the
prize.

"I wish I'd heard it," he said at last.

"Too bad, it's over now," said Gillon, thumping down the
stairs again in his pajamas.

After that there just wasn't a minute's peace. His parents
had both heard the announcement and were clamoring for
Omri to come down for a special bacon-and-eggs breakfast
to celebrate. By the time that was done with, it was too late
to go back upstairs because his train wouldn't wait for him.
Luckily he'd given the food to Matron to distribute, reserv-

ing a special, large (so to speak) portion for Boone in his little house.

Omri just had to go off and leave Patrick where (ever) he was.

There were no skinheads to make trouble in Hovel Road, and Omri got to school in good order, though feeling highly uneasy. He was dead worried about Patrick. What would Patrick's mother say when he didn't show up? And what if he was in some appalling danger, as Omri himself had been in the Indian village, and was waiting on tenterhooks to be brought back?

Omri put his books and stuff in his locker and then went in to assembly. Mr. Johnson, the headmaster, was already on the stage, clearing his throat for silence. More than the usual number of teachers were there too. Several hundred children were seated on the floor.

Omri crept in and sat down near the main doors. He craned his neck, looking for Emma, but he couldn't see her. Hadn't she come to school? He was still looking for her anxiously when Mr. Johnson began to talk; Omri didn't take in what he said, until suddenly, with a shock, he heard his own name.

Everywhere in the auditorium people turned their heads to look at him. Omri sat up straight, alarmed.

". . . very proud indeed," Mr. Johnson concluded. "Omri, stand up and come forward."

Utterly bewildered, Omri rose to his feet.

"Me?"

"Yes, yes!" beamed Mr. Johnson. All the teachers on the stage were smiling, and as Omri moved forward, everyone started to applaud.

Omri found himself being helped onto the stage, and, turning, saw he was the focus of hundreds of pairs of eyes. What was all this? If only he'd been listening!

"Now, it just so happens," said Mr. Johnson, in unfamiliarly genial tones, "that I have here a copy of Omri's story, which had to be kept by the school when Omri entered it for the competition. And what I thought would be really nice is if Omri would agree to read us his winning story as this morning's assembly feature."

Omri's mouth fell open.

Mr. Johnson was handing him a typed manuscript which he well recognized—he'd typed it himself, hunt-and-peck system, in three copies. One he'd sent in to Telecom for the writing competition, one he'd kept, and this one he'd had to hand in to the school office. Across the top was typed the title: "The Plastic Indian."

He clutched it till it creased, swallowed hard, and looked up at Mr. Johnson imploringly.

"Now, now, Omri, no false modesty! Telecom has notified the school that you have won first prize in the intermediate age group—three hundred pounds! What about that, you people?" There was an impressed and envious gasp from the assembled crowd below, and Omri heard murmurs of "Three hundred quid! Wow! Get old Omri, then—millionaire time! Blimey!" And they burst into applause all over again.

"Stand here in the middle of the stage," Mr. Johnson said, maneuvering Omri by the shoulders. "Now then! I haven't had a chance to read this myself yet, so I'm just going to sit here and enjoy it. Well done, Omri! Off you go!"

Omri dithered for a moment or two and then thought,

Hey, this isn't half bad. I've dreamed of this happening! So
he began to read.

The story was based on his first meeting with the Indian, a
year ago when he'd first discovered the cupboard and the
key's magic. It was a great story, and he'd done his best to
write it well. At first when he began to read it, he was
nervous and stumbled over the words, but after a paragraph
or two he hit his stride and began to read with feeling and
expression. He did Little Bear's gruff voice and had a stab at
Boone's Texas accent; when he said something funny, the
whole auditorium erupted with laughter. During the exciting bits everyone sat poised to catch what came next. It was
very satisfying, and when he finished the story and the applause broke out again, with some cheering, Omri felt this
was a great moment in his life, one that he'd always remember.

In fact he was feeling extremely pleased with himself—
not at all a sensation he was accustomed to at school—when
he suddenly became aware that Mr. Johnson had stood up
behind him and was looming over him in a distinctly sinister
manner.

Before the applause had died away, Mr. Johnson bent
down and whispered something in Omri's ear that made his
blood chill in his veins.

"I want to see you in my office immediately."

Omri turned to look at him. He was appalled to see that all
geniality had been wiped from the headmaster's face, which
had gone the color of a wet sheet.

"That story," pursued the grim voice in a hissing under-
tone meant for Omri's ears alone, "was supposed to be an
invention. I have reason to believe that most of it, incredible
as it seems, may be true."

14.

A Strange
Yellow Sky

Doc Brant put his old-fashioned stethoscope back in his
bag in silence.

Patrick, peeping through the frill of cotton lace around
the top of Ruby Lou's dress, saw Boone lying on her bed on a
bright-colored patchwork quilt.

At least he wasn't lying out on the hot desert sand anymore, though it had not been so hot by the time they had
finally found him—it had been getting dark, and Patrick had
been scared they'd never find him at all.

The horse had been pretty useless—it became clear quite
early on that it hadn't a clue where it had left Boone. But
Ruby Lou had been absolutely determined to find him.
Luckily Tickle's many and varied talents included amateur
tracking. With his help, they had finally found the place
where the horse's tracks had rejoined the main trail into

town. This had been made possible by the fact that the horse was wearing some very unusual horseshoes.

"Like some'n from a bygone age," Tick had remarked.

After that it had just been a matter of following them, and when they lost them on some hard ground, Patrick had noticed—silhouetted against a magnificent desert sunset—a tall cactus sticking up on the horizon that he recognized. Soon after that Ruby Lou and Tickle were heaving Boone's unconscious body onto the back of Tick's wagon.

"Sure must have had a crack on the head or some'n," squeaked Tick. "He's out colder 'n last week's beans."

Doc Brant said nothing about last week's beans. He was a man of few words. He just packed his stethoscope away and prepared to leave.

"Well, Doc?" cried Ruby Lou anxiously.

The old man shook his head. "Cain't find nothin' wrong with him. Head's okay. Ain't got fever. Ain't bin shot. Nothin' but a bit o' bruisin' on the ribs, mebbe from when he fell off the horse. Seems like he plumb don't favor wakin' up."

"God pardon sin, Doc—mebbe he's drunk?" asked Tickle piously.

"Look who's talkin'," muttered Ruby.

The doctor shook his head. "No liquor on his breath. Cain't explain it. Just better leave him lay."

When he'd gone, Tickle said he'd mosey over to the saloon to tickle the ivories for a while to soothe his nerves.

"You be okay here alone, Ruby?"

"I ain't alone," she replied promptly, and patted her bosom. "Pat and me'll keep each other company and decide what t' do about Billy, here."

Tickle suddenly drew himself up to his full height of five feet and intoned in an unexpectedly deep, commanding voice, "Don't you go believin' everythin' you see. There's a lot of devil's work in this world! I know it, account of I ain't free of sin myself!" And he cast his eyes to heaven before closing the door.

"D' you hear that? There's a bit of the preacher left in him, even though he ain't held a service since the Dead-Eye Gang went through and burned the church down in '81. That's how he learnt trackin'—trying to chase 'em."

As she spoke, Ruby lifted Patrick out between finger and thumb and set him on a table.

It was covered with a rich—and, from Patrick's point of view, colossal—assortment of feminine fancies: a tortoise-shell-backed hairbrush, elaborate bottles of perfume, a number of sepia-tinted photos in heavily worked silver frames, an ivory comb. . . . Patrick could easily have sunk and suffocated in the scented powder in a cut-glass bowl, and the mirror in its bright enamel frame, above which he could just see his head, was the size of a reflecting skyscraper. The copper hairpins scattered about were as tall as himself.

"Okay, Pat, let's hear from you," said Ruby Lou.

"Who, me?" said Patrick, startled.

"Don't string me no line now. You know what's up with my pal Billy Boone, don't ya." It was not a question. Her blue eyes were narrowed as she looked at him, though her wide red mouth was smiling knowingly.

Patrick sat down cross-legged on a white swansdown powder puff. "Yes, I do, as a matter of fact. But you won't believe me if I tell you."

"Try me."

Patrick told her. "Boone's left his body behind and gone into the future."

There was a pause while she took this in.

"Supposin' I say I believe ya. An' I jest might, 'cause he told me some such tale himself once. Will he come back?"

"Yes. But only if my friend Omri turns the key at—at the other end."

"Into the future, huh? Is that where you come from?"

"Yes."

"What year?" she asked, as if that would catch him out.

Patrick told her.

She straightened up. "Holy snakes! That's almost exactly a hundred years from now!"

She walked about the room for a bit. Patrick watched her. Of course she was rather gaudily dressed, and he supposed she was a lady in name only, so to speak, but when she was at the far side of the room, so he could see all of her, it was obvious that she was very pretty. She was clever, too,

cleverer than all those crazy men in the bar who had started shooting and fighting at the sight of him.

And she was brave, and tough. The way she'd ridden that horse, the way she'd stuck to the search, the way she'd lifted Boone's big body onto the tail of the wagon . . . Patrick admired her. And she liked Boone, she liked him a lot. Patrick wondered if he liked her.

She stopped pacing. "What's it like—in the future?"

"It's okay. We've got a lot of gadgets and stuff, for making life easier. You get about in cars—that's like horseless carriages, very fast—and we've got flying machines. We've got moving photographs that you can have in your home to entertain you. And doctors have found out how to cure lots of diseases, so people live longer."

"Gee. Sounds great! Any drawbacks?"

She *was* clever.

"Well, yes. There are too many people really. They make a lot of mess, and plenty of them are still poor and starving. There's still crime. And there are lots of wars. Not just with guns, and bows and arrows and stuff. There are weapons now—I mean—*then,* I mean—well, anyway, they're much scarier, they could blow up the whole world."

Ruby Lou strolled back to him and sat down. She put her elbow on the table near him (her arm was like a great white marble pillar) and rested her chin on her hand. She fixed her blue eyes on him.

"That's quite a drawback all right. I guess I'll stick around here till my time's up. . . . It gets rough at times, but at least we're too civilized to kill more 'n one or two at once. Say, they ain't gonna shoot any of them big ones off while Billy's there, are they?"

"I don't suppose so."

"They better not blow up my Billy," she said. And the way she said it showed Patrick that she didn't just *like* Boone.

Patrick spent the night cozily in the pocket of a raccoon-skin jacket of Ruby Lou's, which she laid out on a chair for him. She spent the night sitting by the bed watching Boone.

"Won't you be tired?" asked Patrick as she bedded him down after giving him a supper of a few fibers of underdone steak and a crumb of potato washed down with milk from her sewing thimble.

"Don't you fret about me, pal. I'm used to goin' without sleep."

She turned the oil lamp low so as not to disturb him, and he saw her move to the window. She drew back the frilly curtains.

"Sky's a funny color," she said, peering out into the night. "Don't like the feel of the air, neither. Kinda tight-feeling. Hope we ain't in for a big blow."

Patrick slept peacefully. In the morning he woke, with the fur tickling his nose, to all the noises of the town: horses neighing, wheels rattling, dogs barking, cocks crowing, people's voices—but behind and around all this was something odd and eerie. A sort of whining, gusting sound.

Ruby was standing where he had last seen her, at the window. Patrick sat up in the fur and sneezed.

"Ruby!" he called as loudly as he could.

She turned from the window, stooped, and lifted him. Her

hand was soft, except for some callouses as big as watermelons, which must have come from riding. It smelled sweetly of soap—and was trembling.

"How's Boone?"

"Jest the same. Come here and look at the sky."

She carried him to the window. He rested his arms along the top of her curled finger and looked up. The sky, and indeed the air, was a strange yellowish color. Below the window he could see giant people hurrying about. The gusting sound was wind, coming in irregular bursts. It caught at the women's dresses and pushed them along. It blew smoke from chimneys away in sudden puffs, like warning smoke signals. It was disturbing the horses, tearing at their manes, flattening their tails to their haunches, making them shake their heads uneasily.

As Patrick watched, a man's big hat was blown off his head and trundled up the dirt street along with several balls of thistles. The man ran after it. Somewhere a door banged and banged, rhythmically, as the wind began to blow more steadily.

"What is it, Ruby?" asked Patrick in a worried voice.

"I'm not sure, pardner. I just hope it ain't what it might be."

"What?"

"Blowin' up for a twister."

Patrick turned to look at her, but all he could see was the underside of her chin. His mouth had gone suddenly dry.

"You—don't mean a cyclone? One of those black funnel things that—"

Ruby Lou looked at Boone, lying on the bed. She'd covered him with a rug the night before. He looked peaceful and had a good color. His hat, which Ruby had picked up on Patrick's advice, lay beside him.

"Say, that'd be one for the books!" she said with a sudden strained laugh.

"What would?"

"We was worryin' about what might happen to him *there*. What if your friend turned his magic key and sent Boone back t' here—and the bit of him he left behind 'd been just—blowed clean away?"

15.

Interrogation

Mr. Johnson kept his hand on Omri's shoulder all the way to his office, as if he thought Omri would twist free and run for it if he didn't hold on to him.

And he might have done it, too, if he hadn't been half-paralyzed—at least mentally—from apprehension.

He knows! Those were the only words in Omri's head. What was he to do when the interrogation began, as it would in a matter of moments? Lie, deny everything—okay, but what if—

Mr. Johnson thrust him through the door of his office, followed him in, and closed and locked it behind him.

Then he walked behind his desk. But he didn't sit down. He leaned forward and rested his knuckles on the desk and glared hypnotically into Omri's eyes.

"Now, Omri," he said in a clear, deep voice which he used on only the most solemn occasions when someone had done something expulsion-worthy, "you know what I have to say."

Omri swallowed and stared at him the way a rabbit stares into a car's headlights as they bear down on him.

"You haven't forgotten that day last year," he said, "any more than I have. The day you and Patrick were sent to my office for talking in class. The day I went home early because I supposed I was ill, having seen something I believed I couldn't possibly have seen. You remember all that, Omri, don't you?"

Omri felt his head nod.

"What I thought I saw," the headmaster continued slowly, "was two tiny, living people in the palm of a boy's hand. They moved. One of them was dressed as a Red Indian."

"It's not right to say 'Red Indian,' " Omri heard himself say in a strangled voice.

Mr. Johnson jerked his head back. "I beg your pardon?"

"They don't like it," Omri pursued helplessly, hardly knowing what he was saying. "You should say 'American Indian' or 'native American.' "

"I have always said Red Indian and I shall continue to say Red Indian!" Mr. Johnson was suddenly shouting. "I say I saw a Red Indian, a tiny little one, and another figure as well, and they were alive, and I spent *weeks* trying to convince myself that I hadn't seen them, that I'd been overworking, and in the end I did convince myself. Almost. Until this morning. When I heard you read your story," he went on, leaning even closer so that Omri backed a step, "it all came back to me in a flash, and I knew—*I knew* that I was not imagining things after all! I ought to have had more faith in my strength of mind, I ought to have known I am not a man to imagine things!" His voice dropped and his shoulders slumped. "I must confess it's a relief in a way. That's what it is. It's a relief." He took a deep breath and allowed himself to sit down.

Omri was left standing in front of the desk. His knees had gone woolly, and his face felt cold.

"Now then, my boy," said Mr. Johnson more calmly, "let us take a new starting point. 'There are more things in heaven and earth, Horatio . . .' "

"Who?" croaked Omri.

". . . As Shakespeare says. I saw what I saw. They were real. *They—are—real.* That is the truth. Is it not?"

Omri stood dumb. He shut his mouth on lies and truth alike, just stood there, silent.

Mr. Johnson was thinking. A year ago, on the day in question, he had browbeaten Patrick into showing him the little people by means of a threat: to telephone Patrick's father. It had worked then. Perhaps it would work now.

"Omri, if you will not tell me what I wish to know, I shall have to get your parents' cooperation."

Omri's eyes leaped to the telephone. His mind, numb before, suddenly burst into activity. He had not locked his bedroom door because he couldn't—it only bolted from the inside. The cupboard was there. Boone was there. Matron was there, and so were a number of Indians. Unprotected and alone . . . not to mention Patrick, in a deep coma inside the chest. If Mr. Johnson phoned home, his mother or his father would answer, and the first thing they would do was go up to his room. If they believed it.

But they wouldn't. How could they?

Looking at Mr. Johnson, Omri saw the same thought come into his mind. Mr. Johnson was not a man who enjoyed looking a fool.

"Go ahead and phone them," said Omri.

The trap shifted. It was not Omri who was caught in it now. Mr. Johnson drummed with his fingers on the desk, looking at the phone, inwardly rehearsing the conversation. . . . No. He must get the boy to admit the truth first. But how?

Just at that critical moment fate intervened. The phone they were both staring at began to ring.

They jumped. Mr. Johnson, recovering himself, answered.

"Hello? Yes, the headmaster here . . ." He listened, and his face changed. His eyes flashed to Omri, and his eyebrows went up. "Yes. Yes, he is. He's with me now, as it happens. . . ." He covered the phone with his hand and said grimly, "It's your mother."

"Wh-what does she want?"

He didn't answer, just handed the receiver to Omri.

"Mum?"

"Omri? *Where's Patrick?*"

Omri's heart plummeted to new depths in his chest.

"Patrick—?"

"Yes, darling, where is he? I've got his mother here, frantic. Emma's with her." His mother lowered her voice. "She's crying. Apparently she told Patrick's mother that he was spending the night with us, whereas of course he didn't. Now come on, out with it, where is he?"

"I—I'm not sure," stammered Omri. Which wasn't precisely a lie.

There was a silence from the other end. Then:

"Omri, let me speak to Mr. Johnson."

Dumbly, Omri handed the phone back, and listened as well as he could with the blood still pounding in his ears.

"Yes? Johnson here . . . Yes . . . I see . . . Yes, I remember Patrick very well." His eyes were narrowed with suspicion as he looked at Omri. "You want Omri to come home? . . . No, no problem about that," he said smoothly. "In fact I'll bring him myself."

"Oh, no!" cried Omri before he could restrain himself.

"Oh, but oh, yes," said Mr. Johnson. He hung up the phone deliberately and rose to his feet. "Come along, my boy, my—ahem!—Porsche is outside. You can direct me."

Omri directed him to his house. What else could he do? His mind was racing ahead. Patrick's mother—his own mother—probably his father—and now Mr. Johnson. They would all be there, all going at him, going at Emma, breaking down their resistance. All he could think of by way of consolation was, *Thank goodness I sent Little Bear, Bright Stars, and the baby safely back!* The figures were still in his pocket.

Mr. Johnson parked his nice new Porsche (part of an inheritance, it was rumored) outside the house under the big old elm that had died in the Dutch elm disease epidemic some years before but hadn't yet been cut down. It was a good climbing tree, and Omri, in his imagination, shinnied straight up to the top of it in a trice. If only he could be there, on that branch just above his attic bedroom skylight, he might manage to climb in, bolt the door, get all the little people safely in the cupboard, restore Patrick, all before anyone could get there by the usual route. . . .

If only! If only! But Mr. Johnson's hand was back like a steel vise on his shoulder, the front door was opening even before they reached it, and there they all were, waiting. Waiting for Omri to explain!

16.

Panic

"Okay, Omri, where have you hidden Patrick?"

"Where *is* he, darling?"

"Where's my son? Just wait till I lay my hands on him!"

Emma's face was actually the one Omri's eyes fastened on. She looked really pathetic. When she saw him looking at her, she gave her head a little shake, which he instantly understood to mean, "I haven't told them anything." But they'd obviously been giving her a rough time, and Omri felt terrible about that.

The mothers both looked as if they were about to pounce on him; his father simply looked baffled. So naturally it was his father he made for.

"Dad, can I speak to you alone?"

"In my opinion, that would be most unwise," said Mr. Johnson.

They all turned to look at him, and Omri saw his father's face tighten. He turned back to Omri.

"Let's go into the kitchen."

"Can I come?" asked Emma in a small voice, as if she thought they would all start up with her again the moment Omri was out of sight.

"Yes," said Omri. "Come on, Em." He really felt sorry for her. She actually seemed to be trembling, and as they entered the kitchen, she dropped something that clattered on the tiled floor.

They both bent simultaneously, but Omri got there first. What she'd dropped was a plastic figure of a girl in red. He thought for a moment it was Bright Stars' figure, but it was just an ordinary girl. Before he could return it to her, his father got between him and Emma, so Omri slipped it into his pocket.

"Now, Omri, you'd better tell me at once where Patrick is."

When the brain is pushed to its limits, something always emerges. Even if it's the worst possible thing, in this case the truth.

"He's in my room, Dad."

"No, he's not," said his father promptly. "We looked."

Omri closed his eyes and waited, but there was no more. Presumably they simply hadn't noticed, or the little people had frozen into stillness. He opened his eyes again. His father was gazing at him expectantly.

"He's—hiding."

"Hiding? What for? Where?"

Omri glanced at Emma.

"In—in the chest."

His father looked incredulous. "Are you having me on, Omri? He can't have been there all this time!"

"I—I don't know. He was there when I left for school."

"But why? What was the idea?"

"He—he didn't want to go home. Yet."

And then his father said the most wonderful thing.

"Well! You'd better run up and fetch him."

Omri's heart bounded with incredulous relief. Galvanized, he rushed to the door, and Emma followed close.

"And I think I'll come too," remarked his father.

Omri and Emma stopped dead.

"No, Dad."

"No?"

"No. I—we'll go by ourselves." Omri turned and fastened his eyes on his father's. *"Please."*

His father hesitated.

"This is all very mysterious," he said, not at all lightly. "I hope there's nothing going on that you ought to be ashamed of, Omri."

"No, Dad!"

"Okay. Go on. But remember, we're down here, waiting, all of us, and if you're not back—with Patrick—P.D.Q., I'll be up there after you."

They raced, past the little knot of adults in the hall, up the stairs two at a time, all the way up to the attic.

Omri's chief fear now was that, after more than twenty-four hours, Patrick would have come to some harm, wherever he was. What if, when they brought him back, he was hurt, or even— But it was useless to speculate. The vital thing was to get him back, but first Omri had to hide every bit of evidence of the magic.

The second they got into the room, he bolted the door and made for the seed tray.

"Give her back."

He turned. Emma was standing by the cupboard.

"What—"

"I'll put her in myself."

"Put who in? What are you talking about?" panted Omri.

"It's the end, isn't it? You're sending them all back now, and you won't do any of it again because the grown-ups are near to finding out, and it's got too dangerous."

Omri looked at her. Her face froze him. She was Patrick's cousin, and now he saw a likeness—she had the same look Omri had seen on Patrick's face so many times, when he had made up his mind to do something outrageous.

"What are you on about?" he asked sharply.

"I picked out that girl. From my model set. I'm going to make her real, and I'm going to keep her forever."

Omri almost pushed her out of his way. "You're mad," he said shortly. He was still breathless from his run, and from stifled panic—his brain wasn't working well, and he couldn't cope with this new threat.

He bent to the entrance of the longhouse. "Matron!"

She emerged. Her headdress was all bent, which happened only when she was thoroughly flustered.

"My dear!" she cried, her hand on her thin bosom as if to restrain her heart from leaping out of it. "I thought you and Patrick were giants, but some people came into the room who were even bigger than you! I think they were looking for something. I ducked back into the longhouse the second

I saw them, and ordered all my patients to keep absolutely silent. Luckily the giants only glanced around once and then went out again, but oh, dear me, it was a bad moment!"

"You did the right thing, Matron. Now I have to send you back."

"Not a moment too soon! And I think I can fairly say I'm leaving all my patients well on the road to recovery. How will you send them back—the nonambulatory cases?"

"Don't worry, I've thought about that." When the chest was empty, he would just put the whole seed tray, complete with longhouse and occupants, into it; that way he wouldn't have to move the injured Indians individually. But he thought he had better send Matron back through the cupboard in case she wound up in the wrong place.

Matron stepped gingerly onto Omri's hand and knelt down to keep her balance as he airlifted her to the cupboard. She was looking at him closely.

"My boy?"

"Yes?"

"You look worried. Am I wrong in thinking that something has happened to—change the situation radically?"

"You're not wrong, Matron. You—I'm afraid I won't be bringing you back again."

She stepped off his hand into the cupboard. She cleared her throat loudly.

"I can see there is no time for prolonged farewells." She straightened her uniform skirt and checked her pockets to make sure she had all her bits and pieces. Her hand strayed once to her cap, and Omri thought he saw her furtively wipe her eyes with the tail end of one of the floating ribbons attached to it. He knew he would have felt tearful himself if it were not for his desperate preoccupations.

"You've been absolutely wonderful. I'll miss you," he said sincerely.

"Oh, pish, tush, and likewise—" But she choked on the last word and simply put out her hand to touch the tip of his finger, which he extended to her.

"You'd better hurry!" said Emma. "Here, let me do it!" And before Omri knew what was happening, she had shut the door with a thump and turned the key. Omri stood silent, his heart beating, feeling the pressure of time, of all the grown-ups waiting downstairs, and realized he was putting off the moment when he would open the chest.

Then he was aware that Emma was standing there with the key clutched in her hand.

"Now I want my red girl," she said.

"You're not going to bring anything to life now," Omri retorted. "I can't let you. If you can't see why not, then—then I just wish I'd never let you in on it."

Emma's hard, almost Tamsin-like look softened. "Please, Omri. Just give her to me. All right, I won't do anything. Just let me have her."

Omri reached into his pocket. "Right. Give me the key."

There was a moment—a bad moment—when he thought she was going to refuse. God, this was scary! The very people you trusted most could become like strangers in their longing for a little person of their own! It was worse than the way people behaved over gold. If Emma could frighten him like this, what would happen if the grown-ups ever—

Suddenly an awful thought struck him, and he stiffened with horror.

Mr. Johnson! Mr. Johnson *knew.* He was downstairs now, and there was absolutely nothing to stop him from blowing the whole secret wide open! That was what he had come for, and that was what he would do!

No sooner had this thought surfaced than he heard something.

Emma heard it too. Both their heads snapped around to face the door.

"They're coming up here! All of them!" she breathed.

"Oh, God," whispered Omri, closing his eyes in despair. "He's told them!"

17.

The Big Blow

"Quick! Give me the key!"

She didn't hesitate now, but thrust the key at him, snatching the red girl at the same time from his other hand. Omri stumbled across to the chest.

"Bring the seed tray—hurry—" he gasped as the thudding of feet on the lower stairway got louder. He could hear their voices, querulous, anxious, Mr. Johnson's the loudest, dominating their questions.

"—No room for further doubt—biological phenomenon—saw with my own eyes—"

Wait, wait! No time for two operations—do it all at once— Omri opened the chest, grabbed the seed tray out of Emma's hands, and put it in the bottom next to Patrick's feet—he was aware of Emma, leaning closely over him—and slammed down the lid. His hand was so unsteady—they were nearly at the door—that it took two or three stabs before he could thrust the key into the lock. Then he turned it.

What happened next was something he could never afterward remember clearly, and yet would never, ever forget.

The main memory, later, was of a stupendous noise, a deafening roar that filled the room to bursting. But the pressure of the sound was not what threw him and Emma right across the room and slammed them backwards against the wall.

The chest . . . He was to remember seeing the end of his chest. It simply lifted into the air as the lid blasted open, and then it disintegrated. It simply blew outward into fragments. One bit of it hit him in the stomach and knocked the breath out of him. At the same time something large and heavy was hurled and tumbled across the floor and struck Emma's legs.

Then Omri witnessed, in a few traumatic, incredible seconds, the total destruction of his room.

The skylight above his bed vanished first, though he was too stunned to see it go—the glass erupting in a puff of sparkling dust as the violent charge that had come out of the chest roared upward through the hole in the roof. But the hole wasn't large enough, nothing like large enough to channel that black tower of pure force that detonated from bottom to top of the little room.

The edges of the square hole bent outward like rubber for a split second, and then with a tearing, wrenching, screeching sound that could be heard distinctly through the original roaring, the whole slope of the roof disappeared.

At that, everything in the room that could possibly move
—all the bedding, the Japanese table, the floor cushions,
books, Omri's collections, the clock radio, and half a hundred other objects—whirled, in a blinding, terrifying tenth
of a second, out into the sky as if sucked by an inhalation
from the heavens.

That was it. That was all, inside the room. But the noise
had not stopped; it had simply gone out of the house. They
could still hear it outside. A wind to end winds, the most
ferocious, destructive blast to hit England for two hundred
years, was beginning a career which would make news all
over the world.

The first of several million trees it was destined to uproot was the old elm outside Omri's house that should have come down years ago, and now did so, with a demolishing crash, right on top of Mr. Johnson's new Porsche.

The wind then proceeded at high speed down Hovel Road, blowing off roofs, knocking down trees, and wrecking the happy haunts of skinheads—a maverick Texas cyclone, which the weathermen had not predicted and could never explain, on its way to cause unprecedented havoc to southeast England.

Omri and Emma found themselves lying on the floor on the very edge of consciousness. Omri was clutching the thing that had hit him, something sharp that dug into his hands. Emma was clutching something, too. What she was clutching was Patrick.

He alone did not seem to be much fazed or hurt. As the deafening noise began to fade into the distance, he sat up, rubbed his hands over his face and head, and said, "Blimey! Just in time!"

The other two stared at him glassily. He stood up, shook himself, turned—and stopped.

"Crumbs," he breathed, gazing around the shell of Omri's room.

He looked upward into open sky, an angry sky still full of whirling leaves and odd fragments. The broken-off joists of the roof stuck out in silhouette. It was like looking out through the wide-open mouth of a gigantic shark.

"You know what," he said slowly, "I think I must've brought the twister back with me."

"Twister . . . ?" Omri's voice came out thickly, and he found his throat was choked with dust. The air was full of it.

"Yeah. A cyclone. . . . We saw it coming up the street, whirling like a black funnel, throwing huge things into the air. It was just about onto us when—"

His hand flew to his mouth. He turned slowly back to where Omri and Emma were lying.

"Where's Boone?" he asked hollowly. "Where's Ruby Lou?"

Boone!

Omri had, in the panic of sending Matron and the injured Indians back, totally forgotten about Boone.

His brain was working thickly. Boone! Boone had been *here*. Where? Where had he put him? Had he been on the seed tray? No. He had been in the Lego house, in his matchbox bed. Omri'd put him somewhere, at his own request—somewhere . . . out of sight. Out of sight, out of mind.

Omri tried to get up. It was a struggle. Every part of him ached and protested when he moved. He put his hand to the ground and dropped the sharp thing that had hit him, the last remains of his seaman's chest—an angle of the lid with an oblong brass plate bearing the inscription, "L. Bear."

As it struck the floor, he thought he heard a small extra sound, but before he could register it, it was drowned by a banging on the door, and terrified voices.

"Omri! Emma! Patrick! Are you all right? What was it, what happened?"

The three of them froze, gazing at each other. It was Emma who acted first. She scrambled stiffly to her feet and went to the door.

"We're all right! Patrick's here, we're all here, the roof's blown off, but we're okay, and—"

"All right?!" yelled Omri's mother. "You can't be! Open the door!"

"I can't," said Emma. "The bolt's bent."

Omri's eyes raced to the bolt. There was nothing wrong with it. *Brilliant,* he thought admiringly. *She's brilliant. That gives us a few minutes, anyhow.*

"Omri!" called his father in a shocked voice. "What was it? What was that terrible noise? The house shook—like an earthquake—"

"I—I think it's some kind of a freak wind, Dad!" Omri managed to croak. "Did you hear the tree come down? It's gone, I can't see the top branches anymore!"

Mr. Johnson could be heard to give a cry of anguish.

"Tree? Down? My God! My Porsche . . . !" And they heard him rush down the stairs.

"Patrick! Speak to me, speak to me!" cried Patrick's mother hysterically.

"I'm here, Mum, calm down," said Patrick shortly. He was white in the face.

"Listen, Dad," said Omri quickly. "We're okay, I'll take the bolt off the door. You go and see how much damage there is. We'll be down as soon as we get the door open."

"Right," said his father. "He's right. Come on, let's go down. Bloody roof's off—my conservatory must be wrecked—" And he shepherded the women down the stairs, Patrick's mother still fussing shrilly.

A silence fell. It was almost too much of a relief to bear, after all the terrifying uproar of the last few interminable minutes. The three of them stood still, trying to get to grips with things. And in that abrupt and welcome lull, they finally heard something that must have been going on for some time.

"Help! HELP! HE-E-E-LP!"

The voice—a very tiny one—seemed to come from above their heads.

They craned their necks. "I don't believe it! Look up there!" shouted Omri, pointing.

Impaled on one of the broken roof beams was a familiar object. Its mirror was no more, its door hung from one hinge, and most of its remaining white paint had been battered off. But there it was, still there, what was left of it.

The cupboard!

And that wasn't all. Clinging precariously to the bottom rim by both hands, his spurred boots kicking over an infinity of empty air, was Boone.

18.

Red Satin

"Help! Git me down! Save me! Ah'm gonna fall! HE-E-E-LP!"

"How did he—Never mind! Quick, we must do something!"

"Boone! Hang on, we're coming!"

"How?" he squawked. "Y' ain't got wings! An' Ah cain't hold on much longer! It's no use!" His voice swooped into a despairing dirge. "Don't bother none, fellas. It's too late t' save me . . . Ah'm doomed. Ah accept m' fate. Ah jest wish Ah hadn't lived such a rotten no-good hard-drinkin' poker-playin' life . . . !"

Once again Emma was the first to react sensibly—the boys were running around in circles under the dangling cupboard, bumping into each other in their hopeless search for something to climb on. Emma tore off her parka and thrust one sleeve into Omri's hand and one into Patrick's. Then, grasping the bottom edge herself and pulling it taut like a fireman's blanket, she shouted up, "Let go! We'll catch you!"

Boone let go and dropped what must have seemed to him a thousand feet, screaming all the way.

"Aaaaaaaaaeeeeeeeeeooooooow!"

He hit the quilting with a tiny plop and lay there, momentarily stunned. Emma and the boys laid the parka gently on the floor.

"Boone? Are you okay?" asked Patrick anxiously.

After a moment Boone slowly sat up.

"That's all Ah needed," he remarked bitterly, wincing as he felt himself all over. "As if it wasn't enough t' lose mah *hat*, an' git crushed half to death by m' best buddy"—he gave Patrick a dirty look—"I git blown almost up to the pearly gates, and instead o' findin' m'self on a nice soft pink cloud, I'm hangin' out there in space yellin' my haid off with not a livin' soul takin' a danged bit o' notice till it's nearly Too Late!" And he wiped away a tear. He scowled around darkly and then changed his tone. "Say, whut hit this place, anyhow? Musta bin some dynamitin' that went wrong."

"It was a cyclone from your town, from your time, Boone. It came back with me through the magic," Patrick explained.

Boone looked appalled. "Say . . . Ah hope it didn't wreck the saloon!"

"If the cyclone came *here*, it couldn't be there at the same time, so I guess your town's safe. And by the way—so is your hat."

Boone's whole manner changed. He jumped to his feet excitedly. "Ya found m' hat? I sure miss it!"

"It's okay, Boone. It's back there, waiting for you. Ruby Lou made sure to pick it up safely. She knows you love it."

Boone stared at him. "You—you run into Ruby?"

Patrick nodded. Boone's eyes began to glow.

"Ya don't say! Now ain't she a great gal?"

"Yes, she is."

"She ain't one o' your prissy, stuck-up kind, neither—she's a real pal, and purty as paint too!" He heaved a wistful sigh. "Ah wisht she was here now! Y' know," he confided, "when Ah'm with Ruby, Ah never feels sad nor nuthin', an' Ah only cry 'cause she kinda likes me to tell her sad stories. And I kin do without drinkin'. That li'l Ruby gal is as good as likker to a man any day. Better."

"That's the nicest thing a man ever said to me, Billy Boone!"

The sound of this other tiny voice was so totally unexpected they all goggled at each other before turning toward it.

They stared unbelievingly. Standing up on the edge of the bit of the chest lid that Omri had dropped was a tiny figure in a red satin dress and high-polished red boots, with blond hair piled on her head and her hands on her hips.

Patrick let out a yell of delight. "RUBY! What are you doing here?"

"Search me! But the tables are turned now, eh, Pat? Now you're the big 'un, but I don't care so long as Billy's my size. Who's gonna bring me over to him so he can give me a hug?"

The boys dived, but Emma got there first. She took the

tiny figure of Ruby Lou in her hand wonderingly and gazed at her. Then she lifted a shining face to Omri.

"She's mine! It's my red girl! I sneaked her onto the seed tray just before you put it into the chest! Isn't she—just—beautiful!"

"Ain't she, though!" echoed Boone adoringly as Emma gently set her down on the parka at his side and they fell into each other's arms.

The freak storm was an absolute disaster for nearly everyone it touched. But for Omri, Patrick, and Emma, and for the little people, it was a godsend. In one way.

The destruction it wreaked on Omri's home and the neighborhood was so extensive that what had gone just before was simply dislodged from the minds of the grown-ups.

To begin with, Mr. Johnson's precious car was a total write-off. To make matters worse—or better—just as he was jumping up and down beside it, ranting and raving at its destruction, a sizable branch from the dead elm broke off and descended on his head. After that, of course, though he recovered later, nobody was about to believe any tales he had to tell about little live men. (Incidentally, the insurance company refused to pay up for the Porsche because cyclones were excluded in the small print. He would have to come to school on a bicycle, a sadder and a humbler man.)

As for Omri's and Patrick's parents, they'd never exactly believed what Mr. Johnson tried to tell them just before they came rushing up the stairs. And afterward they simply never remembered it. The conservatory had been blown to pieces, the tree was blocking the road, their chimney had fallen

through the roof next door: The whole place looked as if—
well, as if a cyclone had struck it. There was no time even to
think about anything else, once they had made sure their
children were really all right.

The storm had severely damaged the school, which was
closed for several weeks. This naturally caused all those who
should have been learning there profound unhappiness. But
they managed to make the best of things.

Patrick's cottage in Kent was okay, but his mother's
orchard (she had taken to cider-making for a living since her
divorce) had been devastated. The problems this caused
meant she was only too glad to leave Patrick up in London
for a time, while she dealt with them. She never did get
around to asking him where he had been during that fateful
twenty-four hours when he was missing.

So all that was on the plus side, at least from the point of
view of the secret.

On the minus side were the condition of Omri's house, his
parents' distress, and one other thing that loomed larger for
him and the other two—not to mention Boone and Ruby—
than anything else.

As soon as possible, Omri got a ladder and unhooked the
cupboard impaled through its back on the broken roof joist.
He took a hammer and carefully flattened the bent bits of
metal back into place until the hole was almost concealed.
He measured the space for the mirror and went out and
bought another to match and fitted it in. He fixed the hinges
and gave the whole thing a rubdown with sandpaper and

repainted it, after which it looked a good deal better than it ever had before.

But all the time he was working on it, his heart was leaden, and Patrick and Emma—when they could be there—said very little. Each knew all too well what was in the minds of the others.

What Omri was so diligently, so devotedly working on was merely a memorial, a museum piece. The cupboard was of no practical use without the key.

And the key was gone.

Emma had taken over Ruby Lou, and—since Ruby refused to be parted from him—Boone stayed with Patrick, who was living in Emma's house with his aunt. Omri was utterly opposed to this, but he couldn't say much—the little people had hardly been proved safe in *his* place. But he lived in abject terror of Tamsin, or someone else, finding out.

Omri was having to share Gillon's room. So in a way he was glad not to have the responsibility of the little people. But there was cold terror in his heart nearly every waking moment—even though Emma and Patrick assured him they were taking every precaution.

It was evident to Omri that, despite the dangers, or perhaps because of them, the other two were having the greatest fun of their lives. Ruby and Boone were living in an old dolls' house of Emma's, which, if not quite small enough for them (they had to really *climb* up the stairs and come down backwards) contained plenty of things they could use—tables, chairs, beds, and kitchen gadgets galore.

What the dolls' house didn't provide, Patrick and Emma

did. Patrick had fixed them up with a little wood stove (complete with stovepipe) made of a tea tin that had a hole on top of the right size for a real, tiny frying pan, and with this Ruby Lou could do some cooking. They used a special little loo, like a camping one, which Emma had arranged, and every day she brought them hot water for baths, and tiny towels (Boone got almost to like washing). Every day there were new things to make and add. They even rigged up real electric lights that were a wondrous novelty for Boone and Ruby, though the switch was too stiff for them to work alone and they really preferred a miniature, but real, oil lamp twice as tall as themselves.

All this was fine, for everyone but Omri. He felt very much alone and left out. Visiting occasionally and seeing for himself only made him sadder. He longed for Little Bear

and Bright Stars to keep him company. Or even Matron
. . . But there was no way. There would never be any way
again. It made his heart very heavy. And very frightened
when he thought of Boone and Ruby, with them forever,
unable to get home, and in constant danger of discovery.

One day, two weeks after the storm, Patrick and Emma
went over to Omri's house.

"Boone and Ruby Lou asked us to bring them here,"
Emma explained. "They want to talk about the future."

The conference was held in Gillon's room, which, even
though he was not around, was nerve-racking. He might
walk in at any moment—there was no bolt on this door.
Besides, the roofers had at last arrived and were banging
and crashing about, throwing down tiles into the front garden where they smashed on the stump of the tree, and
beginning to remove the broken beams preparatory to putting on a whole new roof. Every few seconds something
hurtled past the window and landed with a crash below. This
meant they might not hear Gillon if he approached.

Omri closed the window and the curtains, though it was
broad daylight, to help keep out the noise. Then he switched
Gillon's desk lamp on, and they all sat around Ruby Lou and
Boone, who were seated on a pouffe made of a large eraser.

"Listen, folks," Ruby began, as they all leaned forward to
hear her. "I wouldn't want to hurt your feelin's none—I
mean you kids've made us feel real welcome, givin' us that
special house and all—but we jest can't settle here. It ain't
safe. Every time a door opens, I git me a heart attack, and
besides, I keep havin' nightmares about them big blowin'-

up-the-world things Pat told me about. Now, we wanna git back home, but Billy, here, explained me the whole thing, about the key gittin' blowed away, and it's real bad news. What're we gonna do?"

Nobody knew what to answer. The silence stretched.

As always when things were *really* desperate, Boone was dry-eyed and steady as a rock. "Couldn't we try some other key?"

Omri said, "I have."

The others looked at him.

"With the cupboard. I've tried every key in the house, just on the off chance, but none of them even fit."

"Sure is a pity, with the cupboard lookin' so new and fine —makes me wanna jump right in," said Boone sadly. Ruby put her arm around his shoulders.

"Doncha start now, Billy, or you'll have me bawlin' too!"

"I ain't bawlin'," said Boone. "But Ah sure am gittin' mighty homesick. It could make a man cry to think o' never ridin' the prairies or the deserts agin . . . or even settlin' his favorite hat back on his ears. . . ." This did cause him to give a deep sniff. "And another thing. How's me an' Ruby gonna git hitched if'n we cain't git us a preacher? T'ain't right, us livin' in that house together, even in separate rooms, when the knot ain't tied!"

Ruby gave him a look that suggested she might not have worried too much about that, but she glanced at Emma and said nothing.

"It looks to me," said Emma, "as if what we'll have to do is just keep trying keys. Old keys. Just keep trying and trying until we find one that works."

Again they were silent. None of them believed that would ever happen. This business was a one off, and they all knew it.

"And meanwhile—what?" said Boone.

"Just keep on as you are—I'm afraid," said Omri with a deep, miserable sigh.

They had something to eat, and Omri—who had a special tea prepared—tried to turn it into a bit of a party, but it was no use. They were all just too upset and scared about the future to enjoy it. At last Emma put Ruby into her pocket, and Boone, with some assistance, clambered to his favorite perch with a leg each side of Patrick's ear, facing out and well-masked by hair. He said it was the nearest thing to riding.

Omri went out with them to the gate.

The roofers had gone home for the day, leaving the front garden in chaos. There were tiles and broken bits of wood everywhere. The front lawn and the hedge dividing the garden from Hovel Road were all chopped up and smothered with debris.

"Dad'll go ape when he sees this," said Omri—and then he stopped.

He'd seen something. Something that in the first second he didn't comprehend, because it didn't belong. Not that bright color. He paused to look closer. The others were ahead of him, starting down the road toward the station. Omri reached up his hand to the top of the hedge.

And then he saw what it was.

He didn't shout and jump and cheer. It was too important for that. He simply stood there with his hand raised, touching it, not pulling yet, just feeling, deep inside him, what it meant.

That narrow bit of red satin ribbon, sticking out between the twigs.

Epilogue
<u>At A Wedding</u>

It was a marvelous, unforgettable occasion. They all came.

Matron—they had to send her back briefly, when they'd explained why they'd brought her, to change out of her uniform. ("Not *remotely* suitable!") She reappeared in a smart navy-blue suit, a snow-white blouse with lots of unexpected frills down the front, and a funny little hat like a crooked flowerpot, with a dotted veil. She was even wearing a trace of lipstick!

Fickits emerged with his sergeant's stripes, which his newly confident manner, after the Battle of the Skinheads, had earned him almost as soon as he returned to his company. When *he* understood the occasion, he wanted to go back to recruit a Royal Marine guard of honor, but he was dissuaded by Boone, who modestly said he wanted things quiet with "jest m' best friends present."

And of course, his best friends had to include his blood brother, Little Bear, and his family.

Little Bear arrived in full regalia—his headdress, his cloak, and all his finery. He had had them on for a celebration of a victory—not a final one, no doubt, but still a victory.

In the two weeks since he had been back in his village, a great deal had happened, which he related to them during the wedding-eve feast. The Algonquins, having regrouped after the previous battle (which Omri had witnessed) had mounted another attack and been repulsed.

"How did you do it, Little Bear? You lost so many men last time."

"Wise chief learn not only from victory. Defeat also teach," said Little Bear, virtuously but vaguely.

"It's strange that when you had the now-guns you couldn't beat them, but without them you could."

"Best use Indian weapons as Omri say." Little Bear's tone was now definitely evasive. Omri was not inclined to press him, but Boone, unexpectedly, was.

"Usin' only bows and arrows, ya beat 'em hollow, eh, Redskin?" he asked.

Little Bear inclined his head.

"Oh, yeah? So ya never even used *m' six-shooter that ya stole off me,* huh?"

Little Bear's head snapped up. His eyes narrowed to menacing slits.

"Little Bear not steal white brother weapon!"

"Well, ya did, 'cause Ah had m' eyes open a mite and Ah seen ya do it. One o' them times ya come to look me over when Ah wuz laid thur, helpless," he went on, while Little Bear became more and more uncomfortable.

"Little Bear!" exclaimed Omri, shocked. "You didn't!"

"Not steal!" shouted Little Bear. "Take, but not steal! Here, I give weapon back!" He pulled the revolver out from under his cloak and thrust it into Boone's hand.

"Real good of ya, seein' y' ain't got no more use fer it, now it's plumb empty. Where's all the bullets, Injun brother?"

Little Bear's earlier discomfiture had evaporated. Now he drew himself up proudly. "One bullet, one enemy!" he boasted.

"Whut? Ya downed six of 'em?" Boone held up one hand and a thumb. "That's right good shootin' fer a beginner." He tucked his gun away in its holster. "Well, guess Ah'll have to reckon Ah *lent* it in a good cause. And *you'll* have to reckon on goin' back t' th' old ways next time."

Little Bear scowled.

"Hard go back old ways after new ways," he muttered.

Bright Stars, with Tall Bear strapped to her back, was also wearing a beautiful dress, covered with elaborate decoration. She rivaled the bride, until Ruby Lou thought of a way to dress up even more.

She persuaded Emma to go and buy a model wedding set that included a plastic bride. Emma was not too happy about this.

"But what are you going to do when I bring her to life? Just rip the dress off her and leave her there in her undies?"

"Nope. Course not! I'm gonna buy it off her."

"Buy it? What with?"

"This!" And she pulled out a minute leather pouch with a drawstring and chinked it against her palm.

Emma's eyes popped. "It's not—gold, is it?"

"Sure is." She tipped the bag a little and something

winked in her tiny hand. "I reckon a few gold dollars ought to pay fer a weddin' dress. Jest hope I like it when I see it made real!"

So it was done. Ruby went into the cupboard after the bride had been brought to life, and emerged triumphant with the dress—a gorgeous thing of white silk and a thousand tiny lace ruffles—over her arm.

"Don't tell me she was at the altar when we brought her!" said Emma.

"Naw! She was jest tryin' on. She told me she didn't like the darn thing much anyhow, made her look fat."

"Cain't all have a figure like yours, Ruby!" said Boone proudly.

The preacher was none other than Tickle. Bringing him was no easy task. There were several false tries. They first brought to life the parson from Emma's wedding models, but of course he wasn't Tickle, he was just a parson, a pallid youth who took one look out through the cupboard door, offered up an anguished prayer, and fainted dead away.

So in the end they went to the model shop with Ruby and looked at every plastic figure in the place till they found a Western saloon scene with a little man at a piano, and Ruby said, "That's him!" And it was. So they got the piano, too.

Tickle was terrified at first. He insisted the whole thing was devil's work and refused to believe it could be happening. But Ruby and Boone took him aside and persuaded him that it was all part of the Great Design, and what really would be sinful was if he left Ruby and Boone unhitched. After a few pulls from a hip-pocket flask he happened to have on him, he allowed himself to be drawn to his piano, and after practicing a few hymns (which he hadn't played since the Dead-Eye Gang had burned down his church), he gradually worked himself into a devout mood and agreed to play his part.

"He ain't much of a preacher man," confided Boone to Patrick, tapping his forehead. "He went downhill fast after they burned his church—th' likker, y' know. Ain't everyone's got a haid fer it like me. But he still got it in him t' do whut's right."

"You ought to help rebuild the church, Boone," prompted Emma.

"Who, me?" exclaimed Boone, but Ruby gave him a nudge, and he said, "Uh—yup. Good idee. Mebbe."

The wedding was held in Omri's room. It was rather dark because the hole in the roof was still covered with a big roofers' canvas. There wasn't any furniture except the built-in bunk. But they spread a sheet over the floor and lit a circle of candles and set everything up the way they wanted it. There was a tiny altar made of a piece of decorative stone, with a single daisy on it, a stained-glass window made of scraps of colored tissue paper with a candle shining through it, and of course a feast of food, including a miniature wedding cake that Emma had found in a rather posh baker's. It was still as big as a table to the bride and groom, but Little Bear would help cut it with his knife. They had lots of crisps crushed fine, and hundreds-and-thousands in dishes made of tiny shells from a necklace of Emma's. There was 7-Up for champagne.

The cupboard was nearby, a little to one side. Its door was symbolically ajar and the recovered key was in the lock. Emma, who had a feeling for these things, had made a little triumphal arch of flowers and a Lego step leading up to the bottom rim. No one mentioned it, but they all knew the little people were going home through it as soon as the wedding party ended.

Patrick, Emma, and Omri had had a long, fraught discussion about the whole business.

"This has got to be the end of it." It was Omri who said it. Patrick knew it too, but he couldn't come right out with it. It was Emma who didn't accept it, who put up a fight.

"It's all right for you two!" she raged. She was nearly in tears. "You've had it for ages. Last year . . . And you've time-traveled. It's not fair, it's just not fair!"

"We've got to, Em. It's too dangerous for them."

"We could keep them secret. . . . We *have.*"

"For how long?" asked Patrick quietly. "Before Tamsin finds out? It's been a pretty near thing once or twice already. Or someone else."

Emma was silent. She was struggling with her tears. The boys were uncomfortable. They understood too clearly how she felt, because they felt it too. More than she did.

"But I love Ruby!" Emma burst out. "I can't give her up, never see her again! It's like—telling me I have to say yes to her dying!"

The boys didn't look at each other.

"I've been thinking about the wind," said Omri slowly.

"What do you mean, the wind?"

"The cyclone. It—it's done an awful lot of damage. It ripped down millions of trees. It practically destroyed Kew Gardens and lots of other places."

"So what? What's that got to do with anything? It wasn't our fault."

"Well, I think it was."

The other two looked at him.

"Look. We—we interfered. We felt bad about the Indians dying, and now we've done this. Don't you understand? Everything that happened—Boone being hurt, the cyclone —even Mr. Johnson's car—it's us. It all happened because we found out a magic trick and messed around with time."

"Good things happened too," said Patrick defensively.

"Like what?"

"We helped Little Bear defeat his enemies."

"Yeah, well, he'd probably have done that anyway, and now we've shown him modern weapons and you see what it led to—him borrowing Boone's revolver because it made killing so much easier!"

"That's going to happen anyway," said Patrick slowly. He, too, had been doing some reading. "White men coming along, interfering if you like to call it that, changing the Indians' way of life. It'd already well begun in Little Bear's time. He knew all about guns . . . We only gave a little push to what was bound to happen."

Omri thought about what he'd read about the way American Indians live now. In reservations, their hunting grounds taken from them, their songs and their gods discredited and lost, many of them alcoholics, beginning only recently to struggle back to their own old ways and traditions and beliefs. After centuries of bad times . . . horrible times.

"I don't want to give that kind of push," he said. "It's got to end."

The other two were silent. Emma gave a deep sniff. Then she said, "But as long as we've got the key, we'll always be tempted."

Omri reviewed the many, many thoughts he had had

about that. He had envisioned himself burying the key, but he knew that wouldn't do. Better to throw it away. Into the Thames, into the sea. He'd tried to imagine himself doing what he knew to be the right thing. But every time, something stopped him. In his imagination he would draw back his hand, the key would be about to fly from it—to sink, to drown, to be lost forever. And he would stop. He could never do it.

The solution he had arrived at was not perfect, but it was the best he could do. It had been born of the deep, long, strong fear he had suffered, and the pain of knowing that they had meddled where they shouldn't and had done a lot of harm.

"I'm going to ask my dad to take it from me and put it in the bank. I'll make a secret package of it, with the cupboard. He won't know what it is. He'll tell them to keep it in a vault and not give it back till I'm dead."

Emma and Patrick stared at him, awestruck.

"Dead!"

Omri nodded solemnly.

"But who will they give it back to then?"

"My children."

Emma spoiled the moment by giggling. The idea of Omri having children—! But then his solemn face took her laughter away. She said, "And will they know? Will you tell them —what it is? What it does?"

"I'll tell them as a story. I won't tell them it's true. I'll leave it up to them. That way it—it won't be quite lost. Only to us. We've done enough."

The Reverend Tickle played the Wedding March as the bride came up the aisle. Matron was at her side, to give her away. Little Bear and Fickits were best men. It needed two, to support Boone. At this last moment he was seized by an attack of nerves.

"Ah cain't go through with it! Ah ain't good enough for her!" he muttered, his face flushed crimson through his bristles. " 'Sides, a man cain't git hitched without a hat—t'ain't legal! Ah'm gittin' outa here!"

And he turned to flee. But Little Bear and Fickits laid strong hands on him and held him firmly until his bride reached him.

Ruby Lou in a wedding gown, with her blond hair down and a lace veil floating around her like mist, was very different from Ruby Lou in scarlet satin. Boone was so smitten at the sight of her that he was struck dumb and his knees buckled. Luckily Tickle had anticipated this, and as he quickly moved from the piano stool to the altar to begin the service, he discreetly passed his flask to Fickits, who gave Boone a restoring swig.

"M' very last!" Boone vowed, but even Ruby, tenderly taking his arm, didn't look as if she quite believed him.

Just near the end, Bright Stars' baby began to cry. Matron tutted and said, "Sh!" But Little Bear and Bright Stars looked at each other and beamed.

"Good omen!" cried Little Bear, interrupting the "I do's." "Baby's voice sign of health, long life! Many hope! Much children!"

And he let out a marvelous baying cry of pleasure that sent a shiver of excitement and happiness through them all.